THE NIGHT
THE NAZIS
INVADED
HOLLYWOOD

THE NIGHT THE NAZIS INVADED HOLLYWOOD

A Novel About Acting, Filmmaking, Politics and About a Mind Control Conspiracy That Is Still Underway

Composed from previously unknown documents

by **Rolf Giesen**

BearManor Media

2022

The Night the Nazis Invaded Hollywood:
A Novel about Acting, Filmmaking, Politics, and about a Mind Control
Conspiracy that is still Underway

© 2022 Rolf Giesen

Cover photos: Stills from *Love & 50 Megatons*
Courtesy of Cornelius Schick

Published in the United States of America by:

BearManor Media
1317 Edgewater Dr #110
Orlando FL 32804
bearmanormedia.com

Printed in the United States.

Typesetting and layout by John Teehan

ISBN—978-1-62933-882-8

Table of Contents

Preface vii

A Brief Foreword: The Magic Spell of a
Cyanide Capsule 1

1   Horsey Rides Again 3

2   The Devil with Hitler 8

3   The Catwalk of Vanity 16

4   Mr. Mouse Takes a Trip 22

5   The Sorcerer's Apprentice 29

6   Burn, Witch, Burn! 36

7   Mortimer the Rodent, or The New Underworld
Order by Grace of Distler TV 47

8   Round-trip to Mars 54

9   The Schnitzel Conspiracy 61

10   V-2 over Distlerland 64

11   The Mystery of the Skull Ring 69

12   The Donkeys of Pleasure Island 82

13   Inside Hitler's Brain 89

14   Götterdämmerung 97

15 Hubbell in the Shoes of the Fisherman............................101

16 Rowboats Dancing in the Moonlight............................104

17 Hitler Competition on German Screens 112

18 Hit the Lukas, or WWII in Outer Space........................130

19 Star-Spangled Eyes..135

20 German in the Blood..140

21 Teutonic Woodstock on the Night of the Witches 146

22 The Black Steam Iron Murders 154

23 A Road Map of How to Become the Next
      President of the United States of America 158

24 Next Exit: Hellgate to Camp Auschwitz 163

    Gallery: A Rare Look Into Nazi Entertainment,
      1933–1945 172

Preface

PASEWALK IS NOT FAR AWAY from the small German village where I am living now and typing this manuscript that is fictitious but not *totally* fictitious: In autumn 1918, a 29-year-old Gefreiter (corporal) was admitted to the military hospital of Pasewalk. The young man was temporarily blinded by a mustard gas attack while serving with The 16th Bavarian Reserve Infantry Regiment in Flanders. He was admitted to a former brick factory and subsequent restaurant 600 miles away in Pasewalk that had been transformed into a military hospital. A psychiatrist by the name of Dr. Edmund Forster treated the hysterical soldier and put the "war neurotic" under hypnosis. The private was healed and dismissed in November 1918, when war was lost, but he never recovered completely from the spell of Forster's hypnosis: Before he believed that he might be the Chosen One, now he was totally convinced. The front had collapsed and with it, for the self-declared Chosen One, a whole world. He was determined to restore the front and never ever would Germany surrender again. Forster later was promoted head of the nerve clinic of the University of Greifswald but suspended in 1933 after the Nazis seized political power of Germany. On September 11, 1933, Forster committed suicide, having been interrogated by the Gestapo. His wife told the police that he didn't own the gun that put an end to his life. Obviously, he did not so voluntarily. Before he died, the Nazis got hold of Forster's papers that described the incredible methods of hypnosis and brainwashing that Forster had applied on that patient in Pasewalk: Adolf Hitler. They were going to turn them into a mighty instrument of mass suggestion combined with secret technology, a process that began on April 30, 1945, Walpurgis Night, the Night Hitler left this world physically with the firm decision that his mind should stay alive and poison the mind of mankind.

This book is based on the idea that this technique of mental control arrived in Hollywood and spread from there like a virus into the subconscious mind of the American audience. It was written around the time the author was hospitalized himself in Pasewalk.

R.G.

A Brief Foreword
The Magic Spell of a Cyanide Capsule

LOS ANGELES FACED QUITE a thunderstorm that night prompting residents to look out their windows to catch a glimpse of the lightning rocking Southern California.

Distler was hospitalized. He felt that he was going to die.

He had smoked too much—although he never ever had bought a carton or a packet of cigarettes himself. His employees were supposed to supply him with tobacco.

Distler soaked with sweat.

He had had a nightmare. A nightmare that haunted him for thirty years, since his first visit to Germany.

He didn't speak a single word German, except for *Gesundheit!*, but in this dream Adolf Hitler would appear and speak to him in German language. And he would understand each single word!

Oddly enough, Hitler wouldn't call him Walter. He always called him *Schnitzel!*

Schnitzel?

"*Schnitzel, haben Sie meine Befehle verstanden und lassen Sie es notariell beglaubigen?*" [Schnitzel, did you understand my orders?]

Distler nodded automatically, *"Jawoll, mein Führer!"*

1

"*Veranlassen Sie alles Nötige vor Ihrem Tod!*" [Then arrange everything before your death and have it notarized!"]

"*Zu Befehl, mein Führer!*"

In his nightmares Distler understood German; he even was able to answer orders in German language!!

When he woke up, he couldn't remember what kinds of orders were given to him.

It was as if he had received a final order from a man who had committed suicide two decades ago.

The Führer's physical shell had been burned to ashes outside of his Berlin bunker, but something was still active: Satan's mind, Satan's brain.

That very Night, right before Hitler swallowed a cyanide capsule and shot himself in the head, his shaking hand pointed on a map and determined a well-known spot where the "1,000-year" Reich should rise again from the dead.

Distler reached for the phone. He learned that the documents were already prepared and just needed to be signed. Distler didn't know what documents but he felt an immediate urge to sign without checking. There was not much life left in him.

1 Horsey Rides Again

THE HERO OF THE STORY you are about to read, however, is not Walter E[mil] Distler, the famed producer. It's a cowboy actor who couldn't even ride properly and therefore hated all horses— although he had a horsey face himself and neighed with laughter about his own jokes that mostly were anti-equine. That's the reason why they nicknamed him Horsey.

In his desperation, he was determined to kill all horses in and around Hollywood, but then Hitler came to his rescue and to the rescue of Hollywood's horses that wouldn't be killed by a Tinseltown madman.

Hitler?

"Hitler might have been a criminal," his new sidekick who rode beside him said, "but he was a brilliant actor. He was the devil, but we can certainly learn from him how to frighten people and how to make them laugh."

Horsey, one of the numerous B movie cowboys who followed in the tracks of Tom Mix, Hoot Gibson, and Ken Maynard, watched his sidekick sternly out of the corner of the eye while his horse watched the rider enviously. The horse called *Crash* certainly lived up to his name. He hated Horsey whom he considered stupid and an idiot. And Horsey hated Crash because the animal looked more stupid than him but wasn't. In fact, Horsey hated particularly those horses that had more brain than him (and that was no big deal). He hated riding at all. Hey, he never longed to become a cowboy actor. He would have loved if the girls admired him as much as Cary Grant, Fred Astaire or Jimmy Stewart. But his face condemned him into the saddle: that dog-gone face of a horse.

When the horse heard the name *Hitler* mentioned, he rolled his eyes.

Horsey sighed. He didn't like that Hitler guy, but if Crash disliked him too, maybe there should be a redeeming feature in that German bastard. Maybe Herr Hitler hated horses too. Horsey didn't know any photo or film footage that showed Hitler riding. He didn't need to ride. He had his divisions of motorized tanks to overrun all of Europe. Hitler didn't go for horse operas. He preferred rattling tank operas.

"How can you say so, Rio? Wasn't that Hitler guy a mass murderer, wasn't he? He would have sent people like you to the next concentration camp."

"Yes, I know—but I'm an *actor* too. There are a lot of secrets to study acting-wise, up there in heaven where all the stars gather…" Rio looked up to the sky. "…but in hell as well where the great villains have their home. Me and my horse, we like to stay in between, don't we?" Contrary to Horsey, Rio Verde (stage and screen name only, all sidekicks had peculiar names) loved horses.

Rio slapped the horse's neck, "You see, I prefer to be neutral and open-minded. But if it's going to further my career, I will leave my position and enter the gates of hell to meet even with Herr Hitler."

Horsey's face became wrinkled. Too much thinking was not his cup of tea. Thinking was something left to horse asses, not to brains like his that could do without worry lines.

But Rio was sure that he should and could learn and improve his acting to get out of the sidekick's saddle and fulfill his ambition: to become the host of a TV show and get tons of fan mail from mostly female admirers.

"Females?" Horsey pricked up his ears. Rio had tapped his problem too.

"Sure, desperate housewives stick on TV. If you're on the tube, you have not only one pussy, you have them all."

"Have them all?" Horsey tried to turn on his brain. "Have them ALL!"

TV was new and hot and might need more comedians and shady-looking characters like them, but it was a taboo topic around Hollywood's movie studios, at least back then, not long after the war.

Suddenly Horsey was afraid that the film producers, even the cheapest ones, might put them on a blacklist if they were going to join TV and betray the legitimate theatrical screens.

But Rio would sweep all concerns aside: "TV is on the success route, Horsey. Nothing and nobody will stop it. No Louis B. Mayer, no Lasky, no Zukor, no Warner, not even Howard Hughes. TV is the *future*—and cinema is the past. They might boycott it now, but in a decade or so these movie moguls (if they're still alive then) will crawl to crosses. TV is going to absorb all of Tinseltown. Mark my words, comrade."

Horsey didn't like the word *comrade*. Was his sidekick a fucking commie?

The director's yell interrupted his suspicion, "Get back to action, will ya?!"

Breezy was a B movie hack who had seen better days. In the late 1920s, he was famous for directing the most hazardous action scenes like the chariot race in *Ben-Hur*. He also directed the flood scenes for *Noah's Ark* that injured unwary extras and killed three of them, deluged by deadly torrents of water in the heart of the mecca of modern sin. That was back in 1929, no good year for the world either. Breezy's risky demands were feared among actors, bit players, and animals. His work on *Charge of the Light*

Brigade racked up so many equine injuries and deaths that new rules were put in place to protect animal actors. Breezy didn't care. He was a boozer anyway. He only cared that his drinking chum Alonzo Jr. was employed in any of his movies. Alonzo drank that much that fruit flies were drawn by the smell and formed a halo around his head. Then he sat with Breezy and Claire, the script girl, and emptied a bottle or two instead of having lunch.

When asked about it, Breezy would laugh it off: "We've enough unemployed male and animal talent here. We don't need to spare it. For each dead donkey we have ten in reserve."

Cameras rolled as Crash, Horsey's malevolent horse, threw his rider off.

A gleeful Breezy knocked on his thighs. He laughed himself almost to death.

"I'll kill that nag," Horsey fumed. "I'll kill all damned horses in this damned town!"

Breezy asked Horsey to repeat the scene—that is, he didn't ask him face to face. The 2nd assistant director was sent over to fulfill the task and he did so rather brusquely.

Again, Horsey was thrown from the saddle. Ten times.

The whole set roared with laughter: the operators, grips, gaffers, and prop men.

Breezy shook his head and called it a wrap.

Horsey stood there, pissed off.

"Think it over, Horsey," Rio demanded when Horsey wiped the dust and rubbed his butt. "The two of us! On the tube!! And I guarantee you: These stupid movie moguls won't even recognize us."

"Not recognize us?"

"Yeah, we get ourselves a secret identity. Like the *SuperBatMan*."

"Like whom? *SuperBatMan*? You mean we have to wear bedclothes and pajamas like they do in the comic books?"

"Much better. When on TV, we'll get new faces. Women will love us."

"New… faces?" Horsey didn't understand one word, let alone two. "You mean… I will not have to ride again."

"What the hell are you thinking off? No more ride, no more look like a… *horse*! I told you: We'll get new faces!!"

"Newly painted? Are you sure?"

Rio smiled, "Tonight, we'll have an appointment, brother."

"Appointment?"

"An appointment with… *destiny*. Read my lips: No more horse operas!! Horses will get out of your way!!!"

"But before that will happen, I'm going to kill these monsters, all of them…"

"Just relax. And don't upset the apple cart."

2 The Devil with Hitler

THIS WAS THE TITLE of a 1942 propaganda movie produced at Hal Roach Studios, a small lot not far from the powerful Metro-Goldwyn-Mayer in Culver City. Harry Eugene Roach was born in Elmira, NY. He took jobs wherever he could find them. He skinned mules in Alaska and drove an ice-cream truck in Seattle before he went to Hollywood to work as a movie extra, eventually found his own studio and make Harold Lloyd and Laurel & Hardy immortal stars of laughter. Humor was with Roach for the past twenty years. Nobody ever saw his name in the credits of a movie but he sure had been around all the time. He was a supreme master in changing faces: the Duke of Duplicators. His make-up wizardry had transformed George E. Stone into a "Nip" nicknamed Suki Yaki, Bobby Watson into Hitler, and Joe Devlin into Benito Mussolini in Roach's *The Devil with Hitler*. Although he ridiculed him in that 1942 movie, Roach had been personal friends with the "Duce" who was a great fan of Laurel & Hardy, as most dictators were by the way, including Hitler, Stalin and Pope Pius XII. And Humor had been the "Duce's" barber, a personal gift to Roach when the two planned a film company called RAM Roach and Mussolini in the 1930s, with a ram as trademark. Vittorio, Mussolini's son, personally came to Hollywood to supervise the deal. Laurel & Hardy were supposed to act as comedians in opera films with their scenes shot in Hollywood while all the big sets were scheduled at Mussolini's Cinecittà film factory outside the gates of Rome. But the gates of Hollywood remained closed to Fascist filmmaking, even with Laurel & Hardy as front.

As a consequence (and thanks to the watchfulness of Hollywood anti-Fascists), Roach lost his distribution contract with Loew's/MGM, a company established by Jews, and had to give up his film plans with the movie buffs from Italy. He was forced to apologize and make that anti-Nazi film. Actually, *The Devil with Hitler* began as a Laurel & Hardy feature with Laurel scheduled for the part of Hitler and Hardy cast as Benito Mussolini. (For the part of Suki Yaki Harry Langdon and Charley Chase were considered.) But then the two comedians left Roach and he had to do without them. Only Humor stayed, who already had prepared plaster molds of the comedians' faces to work his magic on them.

Humor stayed there all the time: when the Roach Studios were transformed into Fort Roach, leased by the First Motion Picture Unit of the U.S. Army Forces to make training films. He stayed when Mussolini and his mistress, Clara Petacci, were executed by partisans near the village of Dongo on Lake Como. He stayed when Roach, after the war, returned and became the first Hollywood producer to eat with the Devil and turn his studio into a TV set.

Humor was a short guy, rather formal and stiff. Unlike his nickname, he didn't have the lively sense of humor that distinguished most of his fellow countrymen. Of course, Humor was not his real name. Maybe it was something like Heberto or Horatio or Umberto. Umberto Rizzoli, a former movie extra seen on screen as early as 1914 in *Cabiria* and other *Maciste* films, someone claimed who needed to know. He was said to have known Bartolomeo Pagano, the muscleman who became *Maciste*, from the port of Genova where Rizzoli's father operated a barber shop.

Whatever his name, this make-up wizard had been a black shirt who participated in Mussolini's march on Rome in 1922 and was promoted the "Duce's" barber (using for his work, of course, a sharp barber's knife, so Mussolini must have had enormous faith in him). But his true background and identity was forgotten since Mussolini had him dispatched to Hollywood, together with a precious Renaissance chimney Roach had admired in Rome. In his later life, Roach, who would die at the age of 100, proudly mentioned the chimney that was shipped on orders from Mussolini to his Beverly Hills home every once in a while, but never talked about his make-up slave Humor. Maybe Humor's life was a mystery even to himself. Some said Humor's father was Italian but his mother—his mother was *tedesca*, German.

His task was to change the faces of film actors and make them work on TV in a way that their contract studios in the film industry won't recognize and ban them.

That way Humor became the confidant of many stars, high and low. By not only using cotton, grease, fuller's earth and false teeth, the usual resources of the make-up business, but completely new techniques and formulas that involved rubber masks and prosthetics, he had helped to turn the images of war-cripples into horrible screen creatures patched up by (mad) science. For that task, Roach had loaned him out for good money to other studios like Universal, Republic Pictures and Monogram. Now he made his services, won during the production of Hollywood's *Frankenstein* and *Wolf Man* series, assisting Universal's Jack P. Pierce, a Greek with the original name of Janus Piccoulas, available for the idiot box, Tinseltown's greatest enemy.

He occupied a dungeon beneath one of the sound stages on the Hal Roach lot that looked like a set from Lon Chaney's *Phantom of the Opera*. He had been there ever since.

While working for Roach, Humor moonlighted at a California company called Rubbercraft that designed specialized rubber parts for industrial uses. This knowledge was new in the film industry and very helpful for screen tasks during the war. Among other things, Humor created rubber eye prosthetics to make Occidental actors look Asian and porous rubber that both moved and wrinkled like real skin. Humor was, more or less, the force that introduced foam rubber to Hollywood. (One of his helpers was Don Post who used Humor's techniques to introduce Over-The-Head masks to Hollywood Monster Shows and for purposes of merchandising and became the Godfather of Halloween.)

Roach loaned Humor to RKO to help design the make-up for Charles Laughton's monstrous bell ringer Quasimodo. By the way, *The Hunchback of Notre Dame*'s director, William (Wilhelm) Dieterle, cast as many German and Austrian émigrés in bit parts as possible. That movie was not French, it was rather German and when the camera wasn't rolling, the air was hot with anti-Nazi and anti-Hitler curses from bit players like Curt Bois, Siegfried Arno, Gretl Dupont, Alexander Granach, Norbert Schiller, Rudolf Steinboeck or Gisela Werbisek. But some of the German-speaking extras weren't true anti-fascists. They were here to infiltrate the émigré scene. Humor knew but kept his mouth shut. He always did. He was in touch with émigrés—and he was in touch, by secret connection, with a Munich surgeon who had treated war cripples and had invented new means of creating artificial body parts and was experimenting with totally artificial bodies. That man stayed for a few months in Hollywood, right before war broke out, and was said to have prepared the nucleus of a network. He was also said to have streamlined Hitler's nose, bulbous at the end and fatty on the bridge, and corrected the Führer's nasal shape by cosmetic rhinoplasty. Some claimed that he even had performed a brain surgery on Hitler's dog.

Humor never confirmed another assertion that this surgeon and brain specialist was indeed a Nazi spy. There were even some rumors that Humor was only a front for this man and that he and not Humor had developed all the original *Quasimodo* and

Frankenstein concepts and was involved in creating America's first robots.

Rio was seated in Humor's make-up chair. Humor made up Rio and combed his hair for his first appearance on TV. He didn't say a word. He was totally involved in his work.

After a while, Rio's face had totally changed thanks to Humor's rubber applications.

Rio's new face looked somehow familiar.

That toothbrush mustache... it resembled Chaplin's screen personality. That strand of black hair. Where had he seen this face before? That heavy nose. A heavy nose? Chaplin's nose wasn't *that* heavy.

"Say, Humor," Horsey tried to start a conversation while he did his best to identify Rio's new face. "Our friend Rio here is convinced that this Hitler guy was a brilliant actor."

Humor cracked a mild smile. But then, from one instant to the other, his face froze. He continued to work and put on some more details. He worked from an autographed photo that he had on his table. While working he checked the result on Rio's face and compared it to that photograph.

Rio was given a brown uniform and an Iron Cross.

Six-fifty sharp Rio was on the tube. Early television broadcasters searched for events that could be shot cheaply. There was no big set, no selected props. Just a black curtain and two chairs. Because videotape did not come into widespread use until the 1960s, very early programmers relied on live transmissions. The little money they spent was paid by sponsors.

Horsey stood behind the scenes and lit a cigarette while he watched Rio acting in front of TV cameras.

Tonight's show was sponsored by the Trapp Corporation. Horsey had never heard of that company before. It seemed to have something to do with sausages and Schnitzel as he saw a girl pass by with a plate filled with these particular dishes.

Suddenly, he felt someone's breath in his back.

"Cancel that cancer stick, will ya?"

Horsey turned around and flicked the cigarette away.

A fireman had copped him.

"What are you doing here?"

"I'm… I'm… a friend of that man…"

The fireman grinned: "Oh, you're a friend of Hitler's? Then you will know that *der Führer* didn't smoke, did you?"

A lightning bolt hit Horsey. Now he knew whose visage had been duplicated on his sidekick's face. The fireman put him in the right way:

It was—sure, that's *Hitler's* face! Horsey blamed himself for being that stupid!!

"Thank you, sir, I had forgotten Hitler's name! Thanks for the reminder!!"

The fireman gave him a quizzical once-over and disappeared.

Rio was brilliant in that makeup. The live audience laughed.

The tyrant who in a speech, addressed to the members of the Reichstag, had announced "the annihilation of the Jewish race in Europe" and had done his worst to fulfill this bitter prophecy.

Rio's Hitler was being "interviewed" by a Jew, one of America's wittiest, snappiest comedians: Groucho.

"Say, Adolf, the last years you've made yourself quite rare, haven't you?"

"But thanks to you guys I'm not completely forgotten."

Laughter as the slugfest began.

"Say, Groucho," Rio's Hitler asked. "Didn't your mother come from Eastern Friesland? Isn't your last name—*Marx*?"

"But I'm not related to Karl."

More laughter.

"Nevertheless, German you are and German you will be till you die."

"I hope this will not be too soon. Otherwise, I would become a spook like you."

"The best members of German people's community have dropped dead on the battlefield of Stalingrad. The *Volksgemein-schaft* was the greatest achievement of National Socialism. Like Christ I sermonized: *Rich or poor, you all are brothers! Therefore, you should love each other!!*"

On the spot Groucho coined the term **Make Love, Not War**!

"But that love did include only Germans I guess—and no Jews like me."

Rio hesitated for a split second. Then, all of a sudden, he acted like a true Nazi, raised his hand in the Hitler salute: *Heil...* His voice sounded dry and throaty. In fact, he didn't act; he **was** Hitler who, although he had committed suicide in the ruins of Berlin, was present more than ever, at least in the new medium of TV.

Death scream, off-camera.

Groucho did a double-take, "Another execution? Why did he have to die?"

Rio's Hitler answered menacingly, "That man had been thinking—and neither should you! Otherwise, you will be next in line."

The audience roared. This kind of sarcasm was to a new generation's taste.

The applause psyched Rio up. He had outpointed Groucho Marx!

Horsey was visibly impressed. Rio was right: The Führer was every actor's dream. If Humor could turn a Jew into a Nazi, maybe he could release him from the curse of the horse ass and change his animal-like face into something that was more handsome. For the gift of a new face Horsey was willing to fuck the movie industry and join TV.

Back in the makeup dungeon, Horsey took the autographed photo that was used by Humor as reference. It was signed by... yes, by Adolf Hitler himself.

On a nearby monitor Horsey could watch Groucho bidding farewell and promoting Trapp's Schnitzel. What he said certainly was disliked by the sponsor (and indeed Groucho wasn't asked to host another Trapp-sponsored TV show):

"Hey folks, *Trapp's Schnitzel* is not uniquely Jewish but I love to recommend provided I have not to eat it. Schnitzel, you know, is a German word although, arguably, it sounds a bit Yiddish. The *sch* prefix is in the same ballpark as the *sch* prefix of Yiddish words like *schmaltz* and *schmutz*. And the fact that Schnitzel is fried in oil means that it is similar to classic Jewish treats such as latkes and sufganiyot, both of which are intended to remind us of the Miracle of Chanukah. Schnitzel also reminds Jews like me and you—no, not *you*, Adolf." Groucho pointed to Rio's Hitler who still stood in earshot and thus got the last laugh, "It reminds us of the manna in the desert because Schnitzel is heavily-breaded. *Trapp's Schnitzel*—German brothers, we love you!!!"

3 The Catwalk of Vanity

IN EARLY 1939, principal photography on *Gone with the Wind* was underway on the lot of the old RKO-Pathé Studios in Culver City without the female lead being cast yet.

There was a huge competition among almost every female star in Hollywood yearning for the part of Scarlett O'Hara, the Southern charm belle. These women would have taken mortgages on their lovers' houses and killed each other just to get that role. Chaplin's wife Paulette Goddard, Bette Davis, Lucille Ball, Joan Crawford, Tallulah Bankhead, Katharine Hepburn, and Lana Turner… a who's who, a big parade of famous ladies competing with each other on the catwalk of vanity.

Considering that, Helen Bertha arrived at the right time. She was determined to take Tinseltown by storm. Hitler had fallen for her, she thought, so why not the rest of the world? She felt powerful enough to break any resistance and was looking for allies in America who might be able to help her win that O'Hara part.

After all, she had a secret weapon. One of her lovers back in Germany was the Führer's secret surgeon. And if he could make that ugly man Hitler "handsome" (Helen Bertha knew the Führer face to face, claimed to know every single whisker), he sure would be capable to turn her "undeniable" beauty into a global screen goddess, into a modern-day Aphrodite to be loved by all kind of people from North to South Pole and vice versa.

In her luggage she had a print of her latest German effort—the two-part epic **Olympia** which featured athletic bodies from all over the world, but preferably male master race bodies from Nazi Germany, contrary to anything that could be considered "Jewish", an odd mix of "Aryanism" and conveyed anti-Semitism. The movie was huge, no question about that: a truly National Socialist account of the 1936 Olympic Games in Berlin, but where was Helen Bertha? The credits indicated that she was not the star but only the director of that show. She simply was not there where she longed to be: on screen herself! Apart from all those powerful athletes, beautiful bodies only, not the war cripple lookalikes from Humor's disgusting horror movies, Helen Bertha's so-called documentary was expected to present close-ups of only *one* lead. And that was (thanks to cameraman Hugo Otto Schulze's transfocator lens) the horrible face of Adolf Hitler with its ugly receding forehead and unhealthy complexion that, as if by mind control, every German considered the most beautiful visage in the world, as (for example) Hanns Johst, poet and playwright, did when he was invited to the Führer's personal Valhalla in 1939.

"This countenance! The whole world knows it. Everybody saw it through thousands upon thousands of prisms and perspectives, from hundreds of photographic, graphic, painted, sculptural endeavors. Millions of human beings saw it, millions gained different impressions.

All interpretations of this face must originate from the eyes—one thinks from the first moment, completely dazzled from the thrill of the counterpart. But longer impression doesn't verify this perception. There is the hair! Neither pictorial nor statuary art have yet expressed its pertinacity and originality. Cheerfulness à la Eichen-

dorff strives against each doctrine. Neither steel helmet nor cap, neither comb nor brush are able to tame what is shaped by wind and weather. Like a cloud it throws a shadow over the face; then it opens the facial expressions by its shine.

The temples are an expression of lithic distance. Like sensitive membranes they rest between ear and eye. These are the loneliest temples I ever saw. They dictate aloofness.

Only heads of great, mental Germans have this outspoken concave form. Here perceptions are monitored adamantly. One looks into the eyes, is welcomed by these eyes but in the meantime these two temples cross-examine you, perceive and check you.

I'm sitting diagonally opposite the Führer. The light from the windows outlines the personality."

Helen Bertha had already portrayed the visage (so divine to German national comrades) ad nauseam in her 1934 Party Rally film *Triumph of the Will* but preferred to bring no print of that stinker to America. *Triumph* was National Socialist pop culture "as its finest". So it seemed to be a proper choice to let a woman compile the picture who claimed to have seen the surface of the earth opening up, when she first listened to Herr Hitler's words: *"Then a huge fountain gushed forth into the sky and fell right back to earth. It was as if the entire surface of the earth was being whipped by a storm."*

On May 1, 1935, Joseph Goebbels, Reich Minister of Popular Enlightenment and Propaganda, had awarded Helen Bertha the National Film Prize for *Triumph of Will*: *"This film represents an exceptional achievement in the film production of the past year. It is closely relevant to us because it reflects the present: it describes in unprecedented scenes the gripping events of our political existence. It is a filmed grand vision of our Führer, who is shown here for the first time on the screen in the most impressive manner. The film has successfully overcome the danger of becoming a mere propaganda feature [sic!]. It has lifted up the harsh rhythm of our great epoch to eminent heights of artistic achievement. It is a monumental film, thundering with the tempo of marching columns, based on iron principles glowing with creative passion."*

To her dismay Helen Bertha realized that in Nazi Germany she had become a specialist in cinematically heiling Hitler and not herself. She would have contented herself provided she was chosen to rule Germany at Hitler's side, second in command so to speak, and for some time she nurtured the absurd rumor that the Führer was mad about her. (Everybody knew that the Führer was only mad about himself.)

In 1939, upon her visit to the United States, the *Hollywood Tribune* published a series of articles titled *How H. B. Became Hitler's Girlfriend* that was written by one of her ex-lovers, Ernst Jaeger, former editor-in-chief of *Film-Kurier*, a German trade paper:

Did Adolf Hitler intend to marry the woman he admired and loved: Helen Bertha? Did the furious tempo of world politics destroy the delicate little plant of a romance?

Jaeger let his readers participate behind the curtains in the second meeting Helen Bertha had with HIM:

"That night ended at dawn," Helen Bertha later told a friend. "We sat in front of the fireplace. He said he would bring about situations which would cause all the statesmen of the world to come to him to Germany. The new world-order would be determined by him. He has reason to consider himself the greatest statesman in the world, and I, too, believe that of him. I have never seen him so upset and excited. He stood before me as though on an invisible pulpit, his hair flying. All of a sudden, his lips came near to me."

But Hitler had already another mistress: Fräulein von Braun. Oh no, not "von". Simply Fräulein Braun. Fräulein Braun was Helen Bertha's greatest rival. Eva studied all the pertinent movie magazines and was daydreaming of a career in Hollywood herself. Helen Bertha decided to show her a thing or two and prove herself in the part of *Penthesilea, Queen of the Amazons*. She had phoned an unnerved Hitler and stuck to her guns until the Führer promised, as sort of a consolation piece for her faithful services in the past, to finance the project out of funds provided by the Party.

Helen Bertha walked on air, "*I had withdrawn to Kampen in Bavaria to write the screenplay. And I had to train myself. Penthesilea was a member of a legendary race of warrior women. As Amazon, I had to ride splendidly, without saddle and backwards sitting on the horse. After I mastered all stunts required, we got to location scouting. Parts would have been shot in Kampen, others, the big battle scenes, in Libya. Roughly hundred girls were being trained. No girls but real females you would believe to fight a war.*"

During research Helen Bertha had found out that the Amazon women were so dedicated of being warriors, that they were known to cut off one of their breasts so that they would be better able to wield a bow. Striving for absolute authenticity, Helen Bertha was willing to sacrifice one of her breasts to the Führer and her art. She didn't hesitate to phone a surgeon and make an appointment.

But finally, Hitler decided that women should stand behind the stove and should not fight side by side with male officers. Helen Bertha was told that there would be no money for such a feminist adventure and so her most ambitious starring project fell through. Fräulein Braun laughed in her sleeve. But Helen Bertha was not the one to give up. If not in Germany, then in America—and if it would cost her both breasts!

Once she had arrived in the United States, Helen Bertha was confident that nobody would dispute her questionable talent. As her first Hollywood spokesman she chose Walter Emil Distler. Yes, Distler. Well, Distler wasn't his actual name. Only the Nazis called him that way as they assumed that he was not American by birth but kidnapped from Germany, from evidently Aryan parents. Till the end of his life, Distler would be handled by that code name.

Helen Bertha knew that Hitler loved Walter Emil's animated cartoons with all those rats, cats, ducks, and pigs and immediately made an appointment with him after coming down to Hollywood.

4 Mr. Mouse Takes a Trip

IT WAS NO SECRET that the Führer was a movie buff.

He had his own cinemas in the Reich Chancellery in Berlin and in the Great Hall at the Obersalzberg Berghof. At Hitler's Berghof residence screen and projectionist's booth were concealed behind a Gobelin tapestry in the Great Hall. Hitler saw everything he got in his clutches. In the evening, after dinner, he watched at least two or more movies, surrounded by his guests. The nightly screenings went often three to four hours. The menu was compiled from films just received from the Propaganda Ministry or on request from film companies. In that way, Goebbels was his master's personal drug dealer concerning illusions of all kind, including movies. If Hitler was in bad mood, a funny movie would enjoy him. Films that pleased him were endlessly repeated; others he didn't like were interrupted after a single reel.

He especially loved to see animation and in his private hours sketched witches, warlords, gnomes, dwarfs, monsters, and evil Pied-piping Jews who kidnap kids, all of them supposed to make an entry into future German movies. *King Kong*, for example, was a movie the Führer saw over and over again in his private cinema. He simply adored that picture. Ernst Hanfstaengl, in the beginning a strong supporter and confidant of Hitler who later turned his back on him and went to America, confirmed this strange passion: *He was captivated by this atrocious story. He spoke often of it and had it screened several times.* Despite Hitler's fondness for that particular film, the giant stop-motion gorilla from Hollywood faced some serious problems with Teutonic censorship before it became a giant hit on German screens, too, released on December 1, 1933.

"I am astounded and shocked," one member of the German Board of Censors yelled, *"that a* German *company dares to seek permission for a film that can only be damaging to the health of its viewers. It is not merely incomprehensible but indeed an impertinence to show such a film, for this film is NOTHING LESS THAN AN ATTACK OF THE NERVES OF THE GERMAN PEOPLE!"*

"It provokes our racial instincts," another censor said, *"to show a blonde woman of Aryan birth in the hand of a black negro-type ape. It harms the healthy racial feelings of the German people. The torture to which this woman is exposed, her mortal fear ... and the other horrible things that one would only imagine in a drunken frenzy are harmful to the German health."*

For the final decision the Führer's adjutancy was contacted: *"In every instance that the film potentially seems dangerous, it is in fact merely ridiculous. We must not forget that we are dealing with an* American *film produced for* American *spectators, and that the German public is considerably more critical. Even if it is admitted that the kidnapping of the blonde woman by a legendary beast is a delicate matter, it still does not go beyond the borders of the permissible. After all, psychopaths or women, who could be thrown into a panic by the film, must not provide the criteria for this decision."*

Thanks to the Führer's decision in favor of *Kong*, the movie was released in Germany, albeit with a warning subtitle that identified it as *Ein amerikanischer Trick- und Sensationsfilm (An American Trick and Sensational Film)*.

Even more than *King Kong* Hitler admired Walter Emil Distler's cartoons. Whenever the kids of his leading vassals were invited over to his splendid Berghof residency, the mountain resort high above Berchtesgaden, he made sure that hot chocolate and cookies were served and at least one or two Distler cartoons shown.

Consequently, Hitler got ecstatic when he learned that Distler and his mother were going to visit Europe and Germany: *"Endlich, endlich haben wir ihn!"* During his Grand Tour, Distler was determined to strengthen ties with European countries and do some research for future productions that would be decisive for the fate of their studio and foreign sales.

The Distlers traveled by train from California to New York where they boarded the *SS Normandie* to England and Scotland, from there to France and by car to Nazi Germany. They came to Baden-Baden and drove through the Black Forest via Freiburg, Ulm and Augsburg to Munich. The Distlers arrived there on a Sunday in July.

In Munich Distler was interviewed by a journalist from *Völkischer Beobachter*, the leading Nazi paper, and asked about future plans.

"We are working definitely on the release of a feature-length cartoon," Distler said. *"It should be finished at the earliest in twelve to fifteen months. This would open wonderful options, particularly in your great country."*

Next afternoon Distler had a meeting with the Board of the Bavarian Film Company, his German distributor. They also discussed the project of that feature-length cartoon that should be based on a German legend or fairy tale. Distler suggested *Snow White and the Seven Dwarfs*. The Board members preferred *Hansel and Gretel* because there was a witch to *burn*: *"Brennen sollen sie, alle Feinde Deutschlands!!!—They shall burn, all enemies of Germany!!!"* There was much laughter. "Push that ugly hag into the oven! Let her burn to death!! Our German children like that kind of gruesome stuff!!! It will make them strong and intolerant. And it will work at the box office," they assured. The kids would resemble a Hitler boy and a Hitler girl who were to be turned into aspiring witch hunters and clean up the forests. "And maybe your artists will consider to give the hag some slight Jewish features? A small concession to the public taste."

"Frizzy hair and a big nose."

Distler was not totally convinced but promised to give this idea some thought.

"But will you have enough talent in Hollywood to handle such a challenging task? Why not produce the whole movie in a German studio?"

"But you don't have an animation department that's large enough," Distler argued. "Most of your animation artists focus on nothing else than short advertising films. Your people might be good but not as experienced as my employees in the States."

"Never mind. We are going to build the biggest studio ever equipped with state-of-the-art technique and place it at your disposal. Our Führer will make it possible. Just tell him what you need. He will get you the best talent from all over Europe. You must know, Mr. Distler, that we have plans concerning Europe. And if you need some Jewish cleaning ladies to wipe the studio floor with a damp cloth…"

"Jewish…cleaning…ladies?"

"If you prefer German ones… Your taste is impeccable. Very soon you will be one of us. Then there will be no more Mr. Distler. Then there will be only Herr Distler. You will not realize the transformation. Don't be afraid. It won't hurt."

But Distler was afraid.

"Maybe," the Germans suggested, "maybe you want to do some research on the project while you are here?"

"But I don't speak any German, gentlemen."

"Don't worry about that, Mr. Distler! We got a charming escort for you."

"But what will Mother say?"

"We will take care of her."

The Germans called in an exceptionally pretty girl and told Distler that Eva was so interested in movies and Hollywood and that she loved all of his cartoon films.

Together Eva and Distler strolled through the city and bought numerous books at two Munich bookstores: Chr. Kaiser located in the town hall and H. Hugendubel. One hundred forty-nine books were purchased in Germany and shipped to Distler's Studio as reference material for the upcoming feature-length fairy tale: books by the Brothers Grimm and Ludwig Bechstein, children's tales, songbooks, books about birds and animals, and reading primers written by Nazi poets.

The names of two female illustrators popped up throughout Distler's shopping list: Else Wenz-Vietor (1882-1973) illustrated eleven books by Germany's favorite children's book writer Adolf Holst, NSDAP member since April 1933. Her colleague Ida Bohatta (1900-1992) had attended the Kunstgewerbeschule, the Vienna School of Arts and Crafts. After the Anschluss, the annexation of Austria, she became a member of Reichsschrifttumskammer, the Reich Chamber of Literature. During the Nazi regime her books were as highly recommended by National Socialists as those illustrated by Wenz-Vietor.

Finally, Eva took a specially bound volume out of her handbag: *Mein Kampf.*

When Disney opened the copy, he found it personally inscribed to him:

Für Herrn Distler
in Bewunderung
Adolf Hitler
[For Herr Distler in admiration Adolf Hitler]

When Distler wanted to return to his mother, Eva giggled: "I got a better idea, Mr. Distler."

They passed a corner and saw two uniformed Nazis beat up a rabbi who was on the way to the synagogue.

Eva seemed to be disgusted but not with the sheer brutality of the Nazi rowdies: "These awful Jews! Always kicking up a stink! They deserve it, those bastards! Bald werden ihre Synagogen brennen und irgendwann sie selbst!!!"

Distler didn't understand the last sentence but it sounded as terrible as it was.

Eva led Distler to Hofbräuhaus, the cradle of Bavarian tavern culture, the origin of tradition and *Gemütlichkeit—coziness*, "You must be so hungry, Mr. Distler. Hungry as a wolf." Distler submissively agreed and asked for the menu.

Eva took the menu out of his hand and ordered beer that was served in a stein. And she ordered **Schnitzel**, "The Führer doesn't eat meat, müssen Sie wissen. His is a vegetarian. But you ... *you* will love that Schnitzel, Mr. Distler."

The Schnitzel was tasty. Distler had never eaten anything as delicious.

From the first bite, Distler felt changed. Suddenly he felt *German*, somehow.

After the meal, Eva offered him a cigarette and lit it for him. Distler inhaled the smoke.

"Our Führer doesn't smoke, Mr. Distler, but we know that you enjoy a cigarette or two."

She put the whole packet of cigarettes into Distler's jacket. Distler felt blessed. They ordered another beer. And on and on.

Next morning when Distler woke up, Eva had already boiled a strong coffee. She kissed him on the forehead and disappeared. Distler seemed a little bit confused but sipped gratefully what was offered to him in a cup decorated with a swastika and the initials *A.H.* The previous night he had drunk too much. That was sure. But where was he? He sat by himself in a lavish dining room. Occasionally, a servant in black uniform appeared and refilled his cup.

Then Distler heard them all *heil* outside: *Heil Hitler! Heil Hitler!*

He was led to a chauffeured limousine and when he entered, he saw in the face of his mother. When they left, Distler saw Hitler's Berghof in all his glory.

The Distlers were chauffeured to Mad King Ludwig's castle, Neuschwanstein, that was built on a rugged hill against a backdrop of picturesque mountain scenery, the symbol of idealized romantic architecture. Work on the building site had begun in the summer of 1868 with up to eight meters of stone outcrop removed to make way for the foundations. The foundation stone had been laid on 5 September 1869 with the building plan, portraits of Ludwig II and coins incorporated in it in accordance with the tradition established by Ludwig I. Ludwig II only ever saw his new castle as a building site. Only 14 (however majestically decorated) rooms were finished before Ludwig's sudden death in 1886. The dethroned King had died at the age of 40 in mysterious circumstances. He disappeared while out for a walk with his psychiatrist Dr. Bernhard von Gudden. A few hours later the corpses of both were found floating in Lake Starnberg although Ludwig had been a strong swimmer and the water where the body was found less than waist-deep. A quick autopsy suggested that the King was drowned but no post-mortem examination was performed on Dr. von Gudden. Commissioned by Prince Luitpold, Ludwig's successor to the throne, von Gudden had provided a doubtful psychiatric assessment on the King. Finding him to be suffering from a progressive mental illness and paranoia, he declared Ludwig incapable of ruling.

When he saw the portrait of the Fairytale King, Distler found that he bore a likeness to him provided he would grow the King's beard.

While he thought about doing so, Distler heard a voice. It spoke to him in German language and he understood each single word:

"Bau Mir ein Schloss, Walter! Bau Mir ein Schloss in Kalifornien!" ["Build me a Castle in California, Walter!"]

This order remained recorded in the back of Distler's brain for the next twenty years—until the time was ripe to look for the architectural blueprints of Neuschwanstein he was given while in Germany and build a copy of the Castle surrounded by a Magic Kingdom on real estate not far from Hollywood.

5 The Sorcerer's Apprentice

BACK TO HOLLYWOOD, Distler, now the living likeness of Mad King Ludwig, received Helen Bertha and her entourage cordially and gave her the grand tour through his studio. He showed the guests how his animated characters were developed and explained his unique technique. He let them see sketches for his new production: *The Sorcerer's Apprentice* starring the most valued hand-drawn star of his studio. Distler's whole empire was built on the shoulders of a rodent. Helen Bertha acted as if spellbound to butter Distler up. In fact, however, she wasn't interested in these silly cartoons and family entertainment stuff like that. She was only interested in herself: claiming what she considered her right and becoming a Goddess, at least on screen.

"You are a genius, Mr. Distler; *you* are the sorcerer, not that ugly apprentice *rat*. How do you call him?"

Distler was shocked that Helen Bertha didn't know his famous cartoon star *Mortimer* by name and mistook the mouse for a rat: *Wherever rats turn up, they carry destruction to the land, by destroying mankind's goods and nourishment and spreading diseases and plagues such as cholera, dysentery, leprosy, and typhoid fever. They are cunning, cowardly and cruel, and usually appear in* massive hordes. *They represent the element of sneakiness and sub-terranean destruction among animals. Just as the Jews do among mankind.* At least that was how the Nazis saw it. No, Distler's rodent was neither a rat nor Jewish.

At lunch, in his office, the producer got on to the Biennale in Venice where his feature-length Grimm Brothers fairy tale version of *Snow-White and Rose-Red* (Distler had decided against *Hansel and Gretel!*) and *Olympia* were screened in peaceful competition. He would have loved to see both parts of *Olympia*. Helen Bertha told him that she had brought a print and asked to call her hotel to deliver it to Distler's studio.

"MGM is interested in releasing my picture in the United States."

"Do they? I'm afraid that *I* cannot afford to see it."

Helen Bertha looked at him in disbelief and asked why.

"Don't misunderstand me, dear. I'd love to see your master-piece. But if I would see this film, it would be known tomorrow throughout Hollywood. My projectionists are members of that damned union. In one day or two the whole town would learn from their gossip. You see, I am an independent producer. I have no distribution and no cinemas of my own. Cinema chains and distribution companies are controlled by those Jewish bastards in New York. It could happen that they would boycott me. They almost did to Hal because he joined the Duce's son in founding a company. No, the risk is too much. It's better to remain a silent sympathizer of Germany than lose it all."

At noon Distler invited his guests to a separate room in the studio canteen and asked what they would like to eat. Helen Bertha voted for a salad. Distler ordered *Schnitzel!*

"I heard there is a so-called Anti-Nazi League that applies pressure on producers like you."

Nervously Distler searched for a cigarette. As the chain smoker didn't find any in his pocket (concerning cigarettes he remained the scrounger till the end of his life), Helen Bertha offered a grateful Distler one from her own brand and put him at ease, "You know, Mr. Distler, our Führer doesn't smoke."

"I know. I've heard that he is a vegetarian too. Eva told me so. In Munich. At Hofbräuhaus."

"Eva?"

Distler was still under Eva's spell.

"What did she look like?"

"Oh, I have her photo."

Distler showed Helen Bertha a photo of Eva naked by a lake.

Helen Bertha was thunderstruck. Distler was still under the spell of Hitler's bitch, her personal rival: Eva Braun!

No chance here! The cards were stacked against her. Helen Bertha had to try her luck elsewhere.

She met King Vidor, the director of *The Big Parade*, an anti-war film, and she met Hal Roach who showed her around through his small lot in Culver City, not far away from the Selznick lot, where *Gone with the Wind* was scheduled to go before the cameras. Helen Bertha was introduced to Laurel & Hardy, to D. W. Griffith who was going to cast actors Victor Mature and Carole Landis (suicide by taking an overdose of Seconal on July 5, 1948) for a dinosaur movie titled *One Million B.C.*, and to Lewis Milestone, the director of John Steinbeck's *Of Mice and Men*. Milestone pulled a wry face. He was also the director of *All Quiet on the Western Front* that was banned in Germany thanks to Joseph Goebbels' efforts

Milestone, born as Lev Milstein near the Russian Black Sea port of Odessa, asked if Helen Bertha had seen his movie. Helen Bertha felt pissed as she had been a witness to the riot Milestone's movie caused in Berlin.

The German-dubbed version *Im Westen nichts Neues* had opened at the Mozartsaal (Mozart Hall), a Berlin cinema at Nollendorfplatz, on December 4, 1930. Seldom was a Hollywood movie expected with such anticipation since the pros and cons of this film had been debated so lively. Three former German Reich chancellors were seen in the audience: Philipp Scheidemann, Hermann Müller, and Wilhelm Marx. There were authors like Alfred Döblin (*Berlin Alexanderplatz*) and Carl Zuckmayer, artists like George Grosz and journalists like Egon Erwin Kisch.

The picture, based on a book by Erich Maria Remarque, was a gritty pull-no-punches look at the horrors of war. Limbs were lost, horses were destroyed, starving soldiers rooted through garbage for food, the troops were ravaged by poison gas and artillery bombs, and few made it out alive.

Goebbels assumed correctly that right after *Western Front*'s premiere, the Nollendorfplatz cinema would let its guard down. So enough tickets were bought at the box office to let the brownshirts in the following day, December 5, 1930, to cause a riot that would bring the Nazis into the headlines of the German papers.

7:00 p.m.: The lights went off in a cinema hall that was filled to capacity. The curtain rose. On the screen the main title flashed. The names of Carl Laemmle, Jewish President Universal Pictures, and Erich Maria Remarque, author, appeared.

Suddenly, people began to shout. The projectionist cranked the sound up, but the angry screams drowned the movie sound down. There they were standing on their seats and in the corridors, the roisterers assembled by Dr. Goebbels, Hitler's deputy in the German capital.

After a while, the screening was interrupted. The lights went on. The theater manager went up on the stage. His name was Hanns Brodnitz. Since 1928 he was in charge of Ufa's premiere theaters in Berlin. Conjuring up, he raised his hands to calm the audience: "May I ask you, ladies and gentlemen, to stop interrupting the screening. Otherwise, we would be forced to stop the film. So please, shift your protest to the streets where it belongs. The majority of the audience wants to see this movie."

Shrill whistles:

„Get down off your soapbox! Down from the stage, Jew! Berlin Awake!! Germany Awake!!!"

In chorus:

Deutschland erwache!!! Germany Awake!!!

The National Socialist members of the Reichstag, among them Goebbels and Pastor Ludwig Münchmeyer, encouraged their followers. Brodnitz left. Applause. (14 years later, Brodnitz would lose his life in Auschwitz). The screening continued, the sound power as loud as possible. But still the machine gun fire on screen could not drown the yelling and screaming of the Nazis:

"We weren't such wimps and sissys. We fought for Germany. A foul movie is this: Sudelfilm! Sudelfilm!! Sudelfilm!!!"

"Judenfilm! Judenfilm!! Judenfilm!!! Jewish film!!!!"

White mice were released.

„Juda verrecke!! Juda go away!!!"

Other patrons were molested. Suddenly someone threw a stench bomb, then a second.

Shrewd Joseph Goebbels succeeded in turning this riot into a triumph for the Nazi propaganda machine. They called *All Quiet on the Western Front* a Jewish smear-film (*Juden-Schmutzfilm*).

In its issue of December 7, *Völkischer Beobachter,* the propaganda paper of the Nazi Party, described the pandemonium with relish:

The screening of this production of the Jewish-Bolshevist underworld had to be stopped. Already during the first scenes of this scandalous movie, there were shouts of protest. Especially disgusting scenes with German soldiers repulsively portrayed resulted in outraged shouts: "Enough", "Such Jewish sass we don't have to put up with." Thereupon, the Marxists present in the audience tried to lash into the National Socialists. It came to a fight, and stench-bombs were thrown, white mice were released. In front of the Mozartsaal, large crowds had come together, among them many Communists who tried to attack the National Socialists.

The Nazis' triumph was perfect when the Superior Board of Censors under the Cabinet Council Dr. Ernst Seeger banned Laemmle's pacifist production for being anti-German.

Milestone thanked Helen Bertha effusively and ditched her.
Helen Bertha didn't say a word. She certainly didn't feel welcome.

Roach personally phoned and drove Helen Bertha to meet David Selznick, producer of *Gone with the Wind*. They were welcomed by a group of protesters holding banners: *Helen Bertha Go Home!* How could they possibly know that she was coming? Helen Bertha said to herself that it was not lack of talent on her part but that the Jews were behind that riot. Selznick and his father-in-law, Louis B. Mayer, the powers behind that movie, were Jews. Only this could be the reason why she didn't land the role of Scarlett O'Hara.

The German trade paper *Film-Kurier* reported about Hollywood's Anti-Nazi League:

An Anti-Nazi League has been established in Hollywood which was termed by Vittorio Mussolini returning home from his research trip a "center of political agitation against the Fascist Idea".

At the end of January 1939, Helen Bertha returned to Europe and was interviewed by a French reporter from *Paris-Midi*:

Three months in America: everywhere lustrous reception except Hollywood where she only was received by Walter Distler, but otherwise was boycotted at the instigation of the Anti-Nazi League.

According to recent reports, for the time being they [the Anti-Nazi League] want to support needy emigrants before, with might and main, they are going to pursue their true objective of launching film agitation against Germany.

After all, they have worked on a film in which Charlie Chaplin satirizes the Führer and hence wants to make a laughing stock of him.

Upon her arrival in the German capital, Helen Bertha immediately stormed the office of the Reich Minister of Popular Enlightenment and Propaganda. Stamping with her feet, she cried and complained bitterly.

The minister smiled inside when he learned that the American Jews had denied her the part of Scarlett. He, too, knew that Helen Bertha's talent was limited. That hysteric woman was a pain in his male ass. But how to get rid of those troublesome, annoying Jews? There were too many of them. And the Hollywood Jews were particularly powerful.

On February 5, 1939, Joseph Goebbels wrote in his diary:

Question if one should remove the American films. I am not quite sure about this matter.

This evening Helen Bertha told me her exhaustive impression which is not pleasant. We have no chance over there. The Jews rule with terror and boycott. But how long?

Hmm, hadn't the former Kaiser, Wilhelm II, now living in pleasant exile in the Netherlands, suggested to gas those Jews and get rid of them for all time?

And once they were gassed and Hitler had won the upcoming war, they would be entitled to brainwash the whole world. He decided to talk about this issue to the Führer. A Brainwash Technology had already been tested in secret Nazi laboratories and on concentration camp victims in Dachau near Munich. It was based on hypnotic treatment applied to WWI casualties in Pasewalk. They began with drugs but then found a simpler way. They were going to gas human brains with electronic imagery. Germany claimed the "world's first electronically scanned television service" beginning in 1935. It worked perfectly. It would spread like a virus.

On September 1, 1939, Nazi troops attacked Poland. On June 22, 1940, the French army surrendered to the German occupants. On December 11, 1941, four days after the Japanese attack on Pearl Harbor, Nazi Germany declared war against the United States. But then the Germans lost battle after battle: Stalingrad, Kursk, the Normandy—and were on the road back.

They also lost the battle of *Hansel and Gretel…*

6 Burn, Witch, Burn!

NOW THAT A BRIDGEHEAD had been established in Tinseltown's leading cartoon studio, the Nazis hadn't given up on *Hansel and Gretel*. It was to be an unofficial Distler animated film production. Officially, Distler was not involved but mentally he was going to supervise the whole show: not in Hollywood but in Berlin where a former synagogue that had been spared from being burned in the so-called Night of Broken Glass served as headquarters of German animation.

To please Hitler, Goebbels was determined to build a German trick film industry. *Lichtbildbühne* and other trade papers agreed with the plans.

Doesn't the German animator have imagination? Does he have only inadequate technical equipment? Don't exhibitors want to see his films or don't they want to pay for them? Or are there other invisible resp. unknown factors? How did it come that Felix the Cat *enjoyed us so much, that cinemas brought us whole series of* Betty Boop, *the spinach-eating sailor* Popeye *or the* little pigs *and have booked them mainly for box office? Was it only a single factor or was it a combined effect?*

Do they think they don't have enough talent or don't they dare to "sacrifice" a few hundred feet of film and the fee for the trick film trainees? Animation stands are relatively inexpensive to buy or to produce in the facilities of a big production company. Camera and lighting equipment one will get cheaply. So this cannot matter. Are the cinema owners the ones to put the blame on? Well, they wouldn't be smart if they would pay good money for stupid, boring trick films but—that is for sure—for good, attractive little supporting films they are gladly willing to pay. The motives are quite obvious! One has not only to rely to film the irrepressible Wilhelm Busch (although he has invented sheer film types) but our fairy-tale characters are numerous; one also can choose animals, for instance a cute terrier, a duck, a parrot etc., give him an attractive name and throw him into all kinds of adventures. In the U.S.A. and England, they have started with well-known comic strip characters as they still run them in the big magazines etc. in inexhaustible sequence. May it be a cart horse or ape, duck or pelican always it has to do with delightful sense of humour, skills and inventive mind to bring the artificial character to life. Sure, we have enough of such men and women among our filmmakers. Let them work, all those who are obsessed by trick film. Then German animation in brief time will be weltmarktfähig *[ready to enter the world market]. Then it will compete—supported by German color film techniques and a German art of music—with Felix and all the other film animals from U.S.A., the "country of the already limited possibilities".*

Goebbels glanced around his staff to find someone who would be capable of handling the project politically correct and coordinate it with the mental workflow coming from Distler's brain that had been forced into line, thus guaranteeing a movie following the Nazi way of thinking. His eye fell on councilor Karl Neckermann, a long-time trusted official of Goebbels. In fact, as usual with Nazi parvenus, he was a complete layman. Neckermann's career was based on accounting, meat and sausages. In Goebbels' eyes, however, this qualified him perfectly for his task as leader of the Greater German Trick Film Company and official producer of the story of those two siblings *Hansel and Gretel.*

Neckermann's biography:

Bank accountant, *Deutsche Überseeische Bank*, Berlin

Clerk in a meat factory in Cologne

Floor manager, *Rügenwalder Wurst- und Fleischwarenfabrik/ Ostsee* (Baltic Sea), another meat factory

Member of NSDAP since 1931

Member of SA, later SS

Full-time head of propaganda NSDAP Gau [County] Pommerania

Personal assistant, Reich Ministry of Enlightenment and Propaganda

In charge of enforcement, Memorial Day 1935

Chairman *Reichsarbeitsgemeinschaft* [Working Pool] Safety Measures

etc.

He was, by the way, not related to businessman and dressage rider Josef Neckermann.

Neckermann clicked the heels and extended his arm: *Heil Hitler, Herr Minister!*

He was given 100 artists and 151 trainees.

Neckermann had great plans but no experience and not a spark of sense but he was a loyal party hack. In the 1930s, wherever Hitler spoke, Neckermann was sent a few days ahead to organize the scene for the Führer and mobilize the *heiling* masses. In the long run, after ultimate victory, the Island of Crimea in the south of Ukraine on the Black Sea was to be transformed into a huge European cartoon factory which would churn out feature-length synthetic films to flood the whole world with Nazi-controlled animation.

Horst A. was one of the first trainees of the new company, *"Everybody was afraid of Neckermann because he was such a radical Nazi. He behaved in a rather nasty way."*

One of the many female employees of Neckermann's company was Ingeburg A. She became a special target of Neckermann's wrath because she made disparaging remarks: *If one watches characters like Neckermann, they are poor psychopaths. Thinking about Neckermann, he had only one arm but that arm he hadn't lost in war. He was run over. So he couldn't proudly claim, That arm I have lost for the fatherland. He was a phony character and a pretender. There were many beautiful girls around, all young and nice to see, who came from fashion schools. He was surrounded by beauties and he tried of course to carry on with them. I remember, once I had cut and taken a day off from work. Result was a gi-ant farce: If this is going to happen again...! If you don't take your work seriously...! Old Neckermann, I can transfer you to the ar-mament industry anytime and so on.* Eventually A. was offered a job as art teacher in some school: *I went to see Neckermann and asked him to get a release from his company that was considered* kriegswichtig *[essential to the war effort].* But she was told that she was indispensable. She said, *I'm getting crazy if I continue to draw witchcraft for another half a year. My brother had just fallen on the front. And I began to rail against this useless outfit. I was summoned to Neckermann, and suddenly he wanted to know if I didn't want to make a trip. He patted my hand.* Miss A., however, stood up and told him in no uncertain terms what she thought, *Herr Neckermann, as a man you are finished for me.* So they kept their documents and she was told that she would hear from the labor court. *Four weeks went by. In these four weeks I wasn't al-lowed to set foot in the company. Nobody was permitted to stay in touch with me: This was a rather depressing time. I couldn't tell my mother what was waiting for me: Armament. Concentration camp. I didn't have a clue. And so I left every morning so that my moth-er wouldn't know and would dally away. When my mother finally learned, she went to see Neckermann: He should hold up that mis-fortune. Her brother had fallen. But Neckermann only said, "This doesn't interest me."*

Immediately Neckermann prepared a report to be forwarded to Gestapo:

The above-mentioned Miss A. declared in summer her desire to leave our studio. A job had been offered to her for the same fee at an institution of higher education in Berlin Tegel as art teacher. She would have to work there, however, for only four hours a day. Her request to quit her job was not approved. It rather was arranged with Herr Horst von Hartlieb—legal department of Universum-Film A.G.—to induce a service obligation if Miss A. should insist to leave. The Greater German Trick Film Company relies on the few skilled employees who are available and who have been trained gradually in-house to finish our kriegswichtige *production of* Hansel and Gretel. *It would turn out to be a catastrophe if indispensable workforces would be lost.*

Subsequent to denial of her request, Miss A. repeatedly made derogatory statements about work and company. She didn't recoil to repeat these statements in the Dürer House where she had been employed previously. As a result, the managing director has talked to her in confidence about three months before Christmas and seriously cautioned her. She was told that she would disrupt the labor peace and that the path she would tread would not lead her into freedom but possibly into a concentration camp.

Shortly before Christmas the brother of Miss A. was killed at the Stalingrad front. Miss A. was in hysterics while in the room of the managing director and demanded vacation because she couldn't leave her mother alone. After some consultation, this vacation was granted to her. On this occasion, she kept saying that she couldn't fulfill her tasks and that we should let her go.

On Monday, after English air raids over Berlin, they talked about the air raids and the resulting damages in the cel department. During this talk Miss A. was reported to have said, "Why is this Saftladen *[dump] not hit by a bomb so that I will be free again." This statement has been testified by the department head, Brigitte Q., Berlin Kaulsdorf, Hoenower Str. 63, sitting next to her.*

Miss Q. had testified that in December the whole department and particularly Miss A. had asked her to degrade the efforts of A.

in the face of the managing director [me!] so that she would get a release. This was rejected, of course, by Miss Q.

After all these statements and for the resulting continuous disturbance of labor peace, Miss A. is no longer sustainable in the studios of the Greater German Trick Film Company. If she would get a simple release, then she would have achieved her goal. We therefore ask to induce her immediate transfer as tracer to an electric company. It would be appropriate if she wouldn't be transferred to Borsig where presumably her father is working as graduate engineer.—As told in our last phone conversation, it has been abstained from demanding more serious steps because Miss A. has obviously suffered a lot caused by her brother's death four weeks ago.

It turned out differently.

In November 1943, the former synagogue that housed the studios of the Greater German Trick Film Company was hit by bombs. During an air raid, the workshops were bombed and burned completely. In November 1943 the Ministry decided to evacuate production.

Concerning the casualties, every hand was needed now. Miss A.'s as well as those of foreign artists recruited from France, the Netherlands and Belarus to finish the *kriegswichtige* [strategic] production of *Hansel and Gretel*. It's anybody's guess what's so strategic about a Grimm Brothers fairy tale but it was a time of twisted minds. Of course, before being hired the foreigners were checked for their Aryan background. As special bonus a return trip [*Heimaturlaub*] was offered. Some foreign staffers used this time for courier services on behalf of various underground organizations.

The new factory was located (of all places) in Dachau, a 1200-year-old Upper Bavarian city near Munich. Dachau, as is fairly well known, was not only the new home of German animation. Walking through the town, from the other side of the street the trick film people noticed some aggravating smell. It was the smell of an old meat factory. Not far away the artists noticed barbed wire fence and living stock wagon drawn by men. A female

French artist learned more when in the so-called Black Express from Munich to Dachau, a distance of roughly 20 kilometers, she got in touch with some SS men in their typical black uniforms. The sinister guys invited her to see what was going on inside the refinement. Now the girl understood that they wore the emblem of the *Totenkopf*, the death's head, for good reason. None of her colleagues wanted to believe in what she had to report when she returned. Actually, the protected area was a concentration camp but they all averted the eyes.

Nearby Moosschwaige, where the cartoonists were now working, was originally a recreation home for artists. The housekeeper was Baroness Carola von Schönburg-Glauchau called Carly: "*German trick film had become homeless. How they learned about the large atelier at Moosschwaige remains an unsolved mystery. Anyway, one day Carly was informed that Munich for a certain time would withdraw from the contract at the discretion of the Ministry of Propaganda to make room for the Greater German Trick Film Company.*

The bunch of German trick film entered with noisy youth. Daily phone calls to Berlin. Many trucks brought animation desks and all the stuff that was needed. Soon architects came to design a studio on a grand scale because the first German cartoon was destined to compete with Hollywood. I was worried: Would Dr. Goebbels' hosts produce propaganda films at Moosschwaige? No, that was not. They worked on a fairy tale, a children's film: **Hansel and Gretel**. *The evil, selfish witch, however, looked horrible, a nightmare with crooked nose, yellow eyes, beard stubbles and greenish face.*"

In charge of designing and animating the witch was Gerhard Fiebig, a graphic artist who once had been trained in a Jewish department store. Now he had become Neckermann's ass-kisser. Fiebig had distinguished himself by drawing anti-Semitic caricatures in his leisure time and drew top salary: "*As directing animator, I got the impression that all male artists during the war were happy and relieved not being drafted, including myself.*"

One that was particularly happy was Robert S., a Frenchman, who knocked one of the girls up. Unfortunately, the girl was the daughter of a high-ranked SS officer.

Studying Fiebig's designs, Neckermann demanded some changes, "Make that witch a Jewish bitch."

"But I did my best to make her as Jewish as possible."

"That's not enough. Make her wear the Star of David so that Hansel and Gretel will have all any right to push her into the oven and lock the door so that she will burn alive. Our kids must know that the Jews deserve that kind of fate. Annihilation is the only language they understand."

Fiebig tried again and this time every Nazi around was pleased: "That's her! We should show this movie at the Auschwitz concentration camp, folks! As warning example! So that the whole lot will know why we are going to kill them and their breed!! They have to die so that Deutschland will live!!!"

Fortunately, the unscrupulous German cartoonists fell behind schedule. In that situation a desperate Neckermann didn't hesitate to ask Eduard Weiter, the commandant of the nearby concentration camp, for skilled inmates who were versed in art. Six inmates were sent to Moosschwaige.

But at Auschwitz they never received the animated version of *Hansel and Gretel*. But at There was an artist at Auschwitz who cared for the hopeless kids and gave them a little hope. Dina Gottliebová was one of Hitler's victims, a concentration camp prisoner at Auschwitz. She and her mother Johanna were first sent to Theresienstadt, a camp in northern Czechoslovakia; then, on September 7, 1943 (with 5,000 other victims), they were transferred to Auschwitz-Birkenau in Poland.

Dina and her mother were holed up in the family camp barracks. About a month after being in Auschwitz-Birkenau, a capo—the head of the camp—brought her some paints to create a mural in the children's barracks.

Supervisor of the children's block at the Theresienstadt family camp at Auschwitz II-Birkenau was Fredy Hirsch (1916-1944), who was also deported from Theresienstadt. Some say it was Fredy's idea to have Gottliebová paint a mural on one of the walls.

A Swiss landscape poured out: mountains, meadows, cartoon-looking flowers, anything to perk up the kids. There were about 60 of them, ages 6 to 16. Perhaps the painting would be a dash of joy in their living hell. A crowd of small ones gathered behind Dina. The children were transfixed. She asked if they wanted cows or horses on the mural. The kids asked her to paint some fairy-tale characters. Right away Dina started creating. In Prague, right before the Germans took hold of the city, she had seen Distler's *Snow-White and Rose-Red*. She worked from memory, "*I wanted to paint the happiest scene I could imagine. The animated film by Walter Distler was very popular in Europe in those days. I had seen it in Prague seven times in succession. I was that fascinated by the animation technique. For that time, it was very elaborate. While I painted* Snow-White and Rose-Red, *the kids stood around me and asked me to paint more—which I did.*"

The children were mesmerized, but Dina was worried what the SS guards might think. She would soon find out. A few days later she was called out and one Dr. Franz Lucas was waiting for her. This was long before her own camp was gassed, but Dina was sure that day was her last.

"*Immediately my heart was in my pants. He asked me, 'Did you paint that?'*"

She admitted that she was the artist behind the beloved *Snow-White and Red Rose* mural. He told her to come with him and then opened the door of the jeep for her—a gesture she found odd.

"*I thought it was one of the usual SS ploys, that it was sarcastic. I thought, for absolutely sure, he's taking me to the gas chamber, or I'm going to be shot.*" Dr. Lucas was the son of a butcher.

Instead of driving her to a gas chamber, the young artist was taken to a gypsy camp. There, a man was bent over a camera with a black cloth covering his head. Dr. Lucas announced that he had brought "her." Dr. Josef Mengele, the legendary Angel of Death, took off the black cloth and swirled around.

"Can you do portraits?" he asked Dina.

Mengele wasn't particularly satisfied with the photographs he took of Roma prisoners. His objective was to prove them to be "genetically inferior". So he was looking for an artist and summoned Dina to paint the portraits, paying particular attention to their skin tone. In exchange for her and her mother's life, Dina obliged and dipped her brush in watercolors.

In a way, involuntarily, Distler and his *Snow-White and Red-Rose* had saved her life. In the children's imagination, the characters she had painted came alive and gave them a bit of hope in their dire situation.

Ludmila Rutarova, another prisoner at Auschwitz-Birkenau: *Dina was the lover of 'Lagerältester' [camp elder] Willy, thanks to which she saved herself and her mother from the gas. Dina was a swell girl; before the war she'd attended art school in Brno, and could draw beautifully. Mengele hired her to draw Roma in the 'Gypsy camp' for his 'research.' It was from Dina Gottliebová that I found out that the Nazis were murdering people in gas chambers in Auschwitz. She told me that she was sure of it, because she'd gotten to see the gas chambers, which she'd also drawn. When I found out about the gas, I cried for three days. I saw huge flames flaring, two meters high.*

Gottliebová escaped the Death Mills and—a whim of fate—in America married one of *Snow-White*'s animators, Art Babbitt. The 60 kids, however, didn't survive. They were gassed and their little bodies burned to ashes in the crematoria of Auschwitz. They didn't need to see *Hansel and Gretel*, the most terrible of the German fairy tales. Another one who escaped was Dr. Mengele who passed away in 1979 in his exile in Brazil. Mengele's infamous career, by the way, started as an assistant to Otmar von Verschuer, a racial hygienist, and Dr. Tristan Todt, a prominent surgeon and brain specialist.

Despite Distler's secret input, *Hansel and Gretel* and with them the Third Reich were doomed. The movie wasn't finished and what had been made (spending millions of Deutschmark) was never shown to an audience. Hitler, Goebbels and other leading Nazis (including Karl Neckermann who hanged himself in the toilet) were prepared to join Robert Louis Stevenson's fictional *Suicide Club*. But they were sure that their idea still had a chance to survive because they had taken precautions in case that they were going to lose the war. They still had their bridgehead in Hollywood. It was located at Walter Emil Distler's Studios.

It was a long-term project to infiltrate all of America via California, brainwash its population by using new media tools and the technique SS scientists had developed, destroy *en passant* the Soviet Union, end democracy and (when time was ripe) flood the universe, the final frontier, with the German Way of Life. The idea was to boldly go and spread the Nazis' brain disease at places where no man has gone before. It might take time, might last decades, might take a thousand years—but they were sure that it would work.

But what was the German Way of Life? Kurt Schumacher, a prominent German SPD politician and enemy of the Nazis, seemed to have understood their master plan when he described Nazism as "a continuous appeal to the inner swine in human beings" and stated that the brown movement had been uniquely successful in "ceaselessly mobilizing human stupidity." The man of the future would be freed from the trouble of thinking and of making decisions of his own.

Gong.

7 Mortimer the Rodent, or, The New Underworld Order by the Grace of Distler TV

THERE ARE NO LIMITS to a rodent of extraordinary will-power. Scientific laws do not apply to such a creature. Everything is possible for such a rodent.

Horsey didn't know it at that time but would learn quickly. The day he returned from Hal Roach's TV set and reported back to the movie location, he noticed that the make-up people put a lot of effort into making that damned horse, Crash, the center of the picture. Crash's new owner Breezy had changed his mind and given the starring part to his animal, and thereby pocket some nice extra money.

"But you need somebody to ride your horse, Breezy!"

"Certainly… not you!"

Round the corner came Imra Van Horn, who was one of many Hungarian immigrants working in Hollywood where he was known as *King Kivu*.

Horsey was stunned, "Imra?"

"Hi, Horsey," Imra greeted him and acted the innocent. "How ya doin?"

Horsey turned to Breezy and protested, "But Imra… Imra is no horse man… He is an *Ape Man*!"

"Who cares? I talked it over with Sam. You're fired!"

"Jungle Sam" Katzman was in charge of Columbia Pictures' B product. At that time, he was known as the King of Gower Gulch. Gower Gulch didn't refer to the location in Death Valley, but to an era roughly located and centered at Sunset Boulevard and Gower Street in Hollywood. It became known as Gower Gulch because it was a hangout of studio cowboys and assorted extras and bit players waiting for a casting call. A variety of B companies set up shop near Sunset and Gower. These penny pinchers lived from hand to mouth. The high mortality rate among these companies led to the nickname Poverty Row.

"Sam said so?" Horsey asked.

"He sure did. He said to terminate your contract. Elsewise, you might give him ulcers. And you know, Sam never gets the ulcers."

That's true. Katzman's cigar-smelling credo was that he never would get ulcers with the type of pictures he made: *"If you were to X-ray every Oscar, you'd find every one of them has an ulcer inside. None of my pictures will be nominated, so I never will get ulcers. None of my pictures ever lost money. Knock on wood—I've never been wrong yet."*

Horsey got weepy but it didn't help. Breezy remained firm and Crash gave him the go-by while Imra took on his low-budget gorilla suit.

Horsey didn't know where to go. In his distress he turned to Humor. He fell to his knees and implored him: "Maestro, please, you must help me!"

Humor sighed. He pitied the unlucky Horsey and took his make-up box to change Horsey's face into something that would resemble—well, not exactly a human, more a humanized mouse. Being a mouse, Horsey looked more juvenile than ever, almost cute, a kid that never grew up.

"You see, we don't need you here. We got your friend Rio."

"Rio?"

"Yeah, but report to Distler. I know that they will not turn you down over there. They *need il sempliciotto.*"

"Il... il..."

"Sempliciotto. That's you. You will fill the bill."

"But... but ... Distler? They are only making cartoons at his studio."

"Not exclusively. They are doing a new TV show and need someone who looks like I made you up. Just go and apply for the job."

Homer was right.

The Distler Board of Directors approved him. They were not overly enthusiastic when Horsey showed up. They seemed to be a little stiff and mechanical. But what counted was that they gave him a contract.

Finally Horsey became a TV star, five days a week, but one that would wear... well... *oversized mouse ears* and host Distler's new kiddies' program: *The Mortimer Mouseketeer Show brought to you by your friendly neighbor who bottles... ups...* on this page no covered advertising or product placements, please.

Okay, it wasn't that great a challenge for an actor to squeak like a mouse (and in between doing promotion for dairy products and beverage imported from Germany), it was no Hamlet or Macbeth or one of those hot modern Tennessee Williams stage characters, but Horsey had fallen from the horse into Hollywood's disgrace and—the money was good.

After a while, Horsey became quite popular—not with adults but with children. Kids all around the country noticed him and asked for his autograph. Horsey even asked one of Distler's animators to show him how to caricature himself with mouse ears so that he could distribute this image widely among his young fans.

Distler's TV show opened with a particularly noisy giant Bavarian Cuckoo Clock followed by an intro song sung by four principals who played mechanical figurines that regularly left the

clock. That song went something like that (and somehow sounded familiar):

> *Onward! Onward!*
> *Clearly sound the fanfares!*
> *Onward! Onward!*
> *Mortimer's Mouseketeers don't know any fear.*
> *Our banner flutters before us.*

> *Into the future we move as mouse for mouse.*
> *We march for Distler*
> *Through wind and weather*
> *The Mouseketeers' banner is the New Time.*

And we all will belong to its New Order.

Then the cuckoo called again.

One of the mechanical singers looked like Rio but that must
have been a delusion.

The tune was composed by a guy from Europe; Austria maybe or Germany. It sounded suspiciously familiar but Distler's
main sponsor insisted on using it. The sponsor also insisted on
having Mickey in the show.

Mickey Trapp was a loud-mouthed, twelve-year-old, blond-
haired nuisance, a real pain in the ass: selfish, headstrong, arrogant, overbearing, and thin-skinned, a bully and a coward in one
person, the type of guy you certainly hope will never ever seize
power, in short: a little s**t. He had a reputation for saying anything that came to his mind, no matter how trivial the subject,
and of course would never admit he was wrong (which was most
often the case). His father successfully imported the dairy products, beverage and Cuckoo Clocks from Germany, Austria, and
Switzerland that financed the show. He also operated an exclusive German restaurant in LA called *Schnitzel Factory*, an insider

tip. Trapp Sr. was a tight-fisted and dour Teutonic disciplinarian determined to toughen up his son to become a ruthless, cost-cutting businessman.

So, there was no way to get rid of Mickey. When he entered the studio, Mickey liked to yank Doris' pigtails and yell, *Let's make America great again, let's cut off all pigtails!* But Doris was a tough one too. She chased her cousin Mickey through the studio and smashed him over the head with her metal lunchbox. It sounded hollow. Like everybody around, Horsey hated Mickey but liked sun-freckled, ten-year old Doris Todt (the kids had all very odd Germanic names in that show: Trapp, Todt, Harriehausen, Hasenfratz-Schreier, Leusekamp). But anyway, Doris loved him.

The objective of the show was to promote Distler's animated films, his wealth of merchandise (including Mortimer tin toys, watches and—believe it or else—toilet tissue) and one special project dear to Distler's heart.

One evening, after the show, Distler himself asked Horsey to meet him at his office. Until then, Horsey had seen the boss only from afar. Doris accompanied him to the Holy of Holies sucking on her lollipop (although the precocious girl would have liked to suck somewhere else). Distler's secretary waved them in.

Prominently displayed in the room was the Star-Spangled Banner. A giant display case was filled with the baker's dozen of Academy Awards Distler had won over the past years and other prizes from all over the world. There was a piano, a bookshelf and on the wall a huge map of some real estate.

Distler sat behind his massive desk that once belonged, so the rumor that spread in recent years, to Reich Marshall Hermann Göring. There had been golden swastikas on each side that Distler had removed, melted and sold to an unknown but wealthy militaria collector. An ashtray on the desk waited to be filled with cigarette stumps. But Distler still had no cigarettes of his own. Each visitor was asked to offer him a smoke unbidden.

Horsey was nervous like he was when he first auditioned for the part of a donkey in a Christmas play at grammar school in Moline, Rock Island County, Illinois. His mouth made some agonized noises. He searched his pocket for cigarettes but didn't find one.

He began to sweat.

Luckily, some animator showed up with a short question. That man had cigarettes for the boss. Horsey felt saved.

Distler relaxed while he inhaled the cigarette smoke with relish and began to cough.

"Horsey," he began menacingly. "Horsey, I heard your fan mail is increasing considerably."

"Hmm."

"Particularly girls love you."

"Yeah, yeah."

Doris nodded eagerly.

"But you seem to have forgotten a tiny detail, haven't you?"

"?"

"You have forgotten that we haven't hired you to do self-promotion…"

"??"

"…but to promote—THAT!!!"

Distler pointed to the map behind him on the wall.

"Me and my partners put money into that show and pay you a sufficient fee to sell nothing else than DISTLERLAND!!!"

In 1953, Distler had purchased 150 acres of orange groves in a small Californian town and was going to transform the area into a theme park that should be worth his name.

Right in the center of the map a replica of Neuschwanstein Castle was painted in.

The Mortimer Mouseketeer Show was just a fundraiser to plug financial holes and rebuild Neuschwanstein in all its Bavarian glory in America. The Hollywood moguls called Distler a traitor breaking their boycott against TV, but Distler needed the TV money badly. The TV major Distler was affiliated with invested $500,000 in the park and became a 35 percent owner, plus guaranteeing loans up to $4.5 million.

And Trapp... this was Trapp's hour... Trapp was given the exclusive right to sell his dairy products, beverage, and Bavarian Cuckoo clocks and open a *Schnitzel* restaurant right in the center of Distlerland.

"All Americans will eat *Schnitzel*!!!" It sounded like an order.

The cuckoo from the Bavarian Cuckoo clock on Distler's office wall cuckooed in approval.

This was the birth of Distler TV and the end of Hollywood's resistance against the new medium of TV. Actually, Hollywood studios weren't that hostile against TV in the beginning. They even had tried for some time to come to terms at least with the new technology and install it in cinemas (until they lost their theatres in some legal act of divorcement). But as they couldn't own it, they started to fight it. They claimed that television, the lowest common Hollywood denominator, was only indirectly show business, that it was mostly advertising business. (Maybe they were even right.)

But Distler didn't care about Hollywood. All of a sudden, he switched to German language.

"*All die Juden-Moguln können mich mal am Arsch lecken!!!* Their time is over!!!"

Angrily he stubbed out the cigarette and asked Horsey for a new one.

Horsey perspired heavily. Again, he searched his pocket in a frenzy.

He needed the money. He needed the money badly because he had found the right girl.

Doris giggled, "Isn't he sweet?"

8 Round Trip to Mars

WHILE WORKING WITH the Mouseketeers, Horsey had caught sight of what he considered an ideal bride. Her name was … no, not Doris. Doris was too young. Horsey liked Doris, but he was no child molester. No, Horsey had fallen in love with Joy: Joy Cory. Joy was… well, Joy was joy, a sheer delight, at least in the eyes of the former "horseman". They had met on the set of one of the *Mousketeer* shows when she came to pick up some of the studio kids.

Like Horsey, Joy had been in B movies. In her brief career as screen actress, Joy had played in a sci-fi flick titled *Red Planet Mars*. She was cast in a small bit part opposite Peter Graves, in years to come better known as the star of a poor man's TV horse opera, *Fury*, that Horsey understandably detested. In that movie Graves was an American scientist who, thanks to the invention of a "Hydrogen Valve", had established a communication channel with the industrious water channelers so far away. And believe it or else: People on Mars aren't aggressive. No, they are not. They even believe in Jesus Christ. Jesus Christ! Hey folks, God is speaking from Mars! Armed with this powerful belief, the Soviet regime in Russia, the hotbed of atheism and religious suppression, is overthrown when the Commies try to stop people worshipping the messages from Mars.

Horsey thought this a brilliant idea: Join the Martians and defeat the red menace of Communism! He went to see the movie five times in three days, not only because of Joy's involvement but for the power of its unique idea. Immediately, he began to see more movies of that kind and devour sci-fi books that dealt with Mars and Martians. And he began dating Joy.

One evening Horsey took his wife-to-be to Funny's Sci-Fi circle where a bunch of young pulp writers regularly met and tried to follow in the footsteps of Jules Verne, H.G. Wells and Luxembourg-born Hugo Gernsback, the editor of the groundbreaking *Amazing Stories*. As a kid Funny had dozens of letters to the editor published in this magazine and even was engaged in a bitter feud with H. P. Lovecraft over one of his pulp stories.

Horsey was sure that Joy, as part of the most important sci-fi picture he had ever seen, would be recognized on the spot, a Hollywood celebrity, but nobody seemed to care about women or the B picture she was involved with.

At that time Funny lived at Sherbourne Drive in Los Angeles. His home was crammed with books, papers, photos, documents, artwork, and all kind of trash, including horrific masks, creature claws, toys and deteriorating props from low-budget films. He liked to name his home the Sanctuary of Perpetual Halloween. Funny was tall, handsome, he wore futuristic glasses but you may call him a little weird. Funny (in his grave) wouldn't mind. He liked weirdos, foremost himself. Under his moustache glowed a perennial smile. When he received guests, he liked to wear an original Dracula cape that the declared teetotaler had borrowed from Béla Lugosi, the Hungarian alcoholic actor, and later forgot to return to the owner who had to be buried in another cape anyway.

This evening, one year before his death, Lugosi was present himself. He sat down in a highly comfortable wooden funeral coffin that Funny had saved from Universal's studio junk: bow tie, breast pocket handkerchief, immaculately dressed, just the old-school European gentleman but smelling of beer and bourbon, watching the young people while he smoked a cigar inside the coffin. When one tried to talk to him, he nodded friendly and waved his hand. You could be sure that he hadn't understood a word, not because he had problems with the English language (he sure had when he first arrived in the United States in 1923 and was famous for his thick Hungarian accent), but because he was almost deaf. And he couldn't see as well but refused to wear glasses in public, so he was as blind as the proverbial bat.

He sat there quietly in his coffin, the shell of his former self although daydreaming of a comeback in a stereoscopic 3D vampire pic, with all the folk around him making a nuisance of themselves. Occasionally, one mindless guest would place his glass or put out a cigarette on the rim of the casket. Béla's new wife, his fifth one whom he had married in 1955 after his release from a much-publicized drug cure (for about ten years the old man was medically addicted to morphine like Göring was), didn't seem much interested in her husband anymore and flirted with some young writers.

Funny used Béla as an icon to boost his own (weak) ego. He was like Frankenstein's creature, taking parts from different movie stars. His hairstyle and mustache were inspired by actor Warren William, his signature by actress Kay Francis, he followed Clark Gable's example and didn't wear undershirts. He had left University after one semester to pursue a career as a writer but when he realized that he was more a punster than a romancer, he decided to become a literary agent to all this aspiring sci-fi talent. There were lots of magazines around eager to publish short stories by Ray Bradbury, Robert Bloch or some of the still unknowns who frequented Funny's home.

Robert Anson Heinlein was already a real pro. Heinlein liked to talk politics. To him that meant stationing atomic rockets on the *Moon* as soon as possible. He talked about it in a way as if it was like going to buy groceries at some store round the corner. Heinlein was raised in the Bible Belt and graduated from the Naval Academy. One of his juvenile novels featuring Young Rocket Engineers had been turned into a major movie some years ago. Originally, it dealt with three teenagers who volunteer to assist a scientist uncle in building a rocket to the moon where they encounter *Space Nazis*. One of Distler's producer friends, George Pal, had changed the title for the screen version into *Destination Moon*, replaced the teenagers with adults and, on advice by Distler, took out the Nazis. No, he didn't actually replace the Nazis with Soviets. That would have been too simple. Soviets on the Moon. Incredible. But what they considered the *invisible* danger of Soviet communism would be felt on the surface of the Moon all time. These were the days of Joseph McCarthy's witch hunt. On Earth they would hunt red witches and Communist warlocks—but no more Nazis. (Instead, they learned from the Nazis. McCarthy seemed to regret that he couldn't burn them, like the Nazis did at Auschwitz and other camps). But once their imagination set foot on the Moon, they felt ready to become Masters of the Universe. The future was theirs. It didn't belong to Marxists and Commies.

At least on the screen the space race was early on, and Cold War was expected to get hot all the time.

Horsey was in awe of Heinlein and absorbed his ideas. In his opinion, there was only one downer. It shouldn't have been *Destination Moon*. It should have been *Destination Mars*!!!

The only other woman around was Funny's wife, a stout German-born librarian. Béla complained to her about his new wife in German language, "*Sie schlägt mich. Sie prügelt mich jede Nacht. Ich habe Angst vor ihr. Ich habe vor ihr mehr Angst als vor dem Tod.*"

Funny's wife tried to console the old man, "*Der Tod wird bestimmt gnädiger zu Ihnen sein als diese Frau.*"

Béla replied gratefully, "*Meinen Sie wirklich? Gott segne Sie, Gnädigste.*"

On screen Béla had been a vampire, in real life he was raised in Roman Catholic tradition and feared Death: Bless him!

In the meantime, the attention shifted from Heinlein and yesteryear's horror to Hubbell who had worked his way up from the lowest depths of pulp writing, the scum of scribblers, to a person who claimed to revolutionize psychology and transform it into a technology of the future. Hubbell was going to introduce his newest gadget, an electrolytic psychometer: *ELPSY*. Well, it was nothing else than a crude lie detector, but Hubbel tried to convince the circle that this device would enable an auditor to *see* the very thoughts of a person.

One year ago, Hubbell had found the basic building instructions for a homemade electric lie detector in a Scouting Magazine for boys.

With such a device, he read, one could mystify friends by exposing falsehoods: *Hundreds of tests by the writer have proved its meter to indicate correctly about eighty percent of the time, and that is sufficient to get a lot of laughs at any party.*

The cost need not exceed $2.50. A three-element radio tube (No. 45) is used in the circuit. The other parts required are a socket, 45-volt "B" battery with a 22 ½-volt tap, two 1.5-volt dry cells (connected in series), two cheap laboratory test prods, and an inexpensive milliammeter. A 0-15 milliammeter was employed by the writer of the article, but one with higher readings is preferable because the readings are often near the 15-milliampere mark. A small rheostat can be placed in series with the milliammeter to reduce the readings, if preferred.

The parts may be mounted in any convenient way. It pays, however, to design the box or cabinet so as to look as impressive as possible for its psychological effect.

AHA! Quickly Hubbell added a few gadgets that looked good to him and light bulbs.

The 45 volts applied to the plate of the tube through the milliammeter are enough to produce a current reading of about 10 milliamperes. By holding one of the test prods in each hand, the subject connects the 22 ½—volt tap of the battery to the grid of the tube. As the pressure of the hands upon the test prods increases, the resistance at this point decreases, thus permitting a greater flow of grid voltage. This causes a higher milliampere reading, which indicates increased tension on the part of the subject.

Not the slightest hint as to how the detector works must be given to the person being tested. He or she should merely be instructed to hold the metal end of a test prod in each hand with a light, comfortable grip. The box should face the questioner so that the other person cannot see the reading of the milliammeter.

And all for less than $2.50!

One way of using the device is to tell a man to write down the names of five girls, including that of his wife or sweetheart. He is then to answer "No" to each question, such as "Is it Ruth?", "Is it Grace?", and so on. Involuntarily he will grip the test prods when he says "No" to the right name.

Easy peasy!

Bear in mind that the questions should be planned in advance and asked fairly rapidly so as to catch the subject unawares and startle him sufficiently to make him grip the prods tighter in his effort to control himself and lie convincingly.

As Hubbell was no craftsman or hobbyist, he invited two boys to assemble the pieces for him and as recompense for their efforts donated two glasses of lemonade (from one bottle).

Of course, the later models were a little more sophisticated than the prototype as they were supposed to read how polluted a soul was.

Hubbell had invented a fancy name for his technique: *Macro-Dynatism.* He invited Joy, Horsey's actress friend, to act as human guinea pig in front of all those pulp writers.

Horsey watched it jealously and tried to ridicule Hubbell's "invention" through interjections. The others darted malignant glances.

But Joy felt somehow "illuminated". Her mind, she confirmed to the stunning audience, had been uplifted. It sure would help her to audition for a part in another B movie titled ***Frankenstein's Granddaughter***, a black-and-white cheapy, just a few days of indoor shooting, not much dialogue.

"My technology," Hubbell predicted, "will transform you into America's most important woman."

Horsey felt like an idiot. Why did he bring Joy here? Now he had a rival for her favor. He had to prove that only he, Horsey, would be capable to make Joy a First Lady.

First Lady?

That meant that he would have to become President of the United States of America!

His thoughts were interrupted by Béla's screams. The drunk actor had dropped off in his casket with a burning cigar. There was much smoke and hoopla.

Funny suggested to Béla to better cancel that cancer stick.

9 The Schnitzel Conspiracy

AT FIRST, HORSEY didn't find the place and cruised around aimlessly. Joy got impatient. She had begun to compare Horsey with males who she considered more perfect.

"Whom do you mean?"

"Mr. Hubbell for instance."

"Can't you stop mentioning that bouncer's name. It's annoying, Joy. You're *my* girl, aren't you?"

"We'll see."

Quivering with conflicting emotions, Horsey mixed up forward and reverse gear and almost caused an accident with another vehicle.

When he finally found the correct address and parked his car in the vicinity, he stood in disbelief. Trapp's exclusive Schnitzel Factory looked like Poe's *House of Usher*: an eerie place, damn creepy, surrounded by a diseased atmosphere and rotten trees, deteriorating, the whole exterior overspread by minute fungi. The eye of a scrutinizing observer might have discovered a barely perceptible fissure which extended from the roof of the building in front. The vestibule was dusty and disintegrating. Only one of Lugosi's undead vampire figures would have felt comfortable in such a surrounding.

That was supposed to be a restaurant?

Horsey was apprehensive and hesitant.

The doormat read *Willkommen—Welcome*, but Horsey didn't feel welcome. Joy suggested they leave on the spot.

No, Horsey thought: I am going to prove to her that I'm brave. And anyway, I'm hungry too.

"We're here to eat and we *will* eat!"

When they finally overcame their fear and entered, they heard a

Gong.

A hunchback appeared.

Horsey didn't believe his eyes.

Was this the basement of Notre-Dame de Paris or a hoax?

In some distance he recognized people eating.

He calmed down: "See, Honey, I told you. This is a restaurant."

After a while, out of the darkness, a bull-necked waiter turned up: "*Schnitzel?*"

Horsey was so surprised that he just nodded.

"And for the lady?"

"*The lady will have a salad à la maison.*"

It wasn't Horsey who said that.

Horsey knew that uncomfortable voice. Why, of all places, he must show up right here.

Joy looked at the other man. She was all eyes and totally enchanted.

The waiter vanished and returned with a salad and an XXL cutlet.

Schnitzel is perhaps the most famous Viennese dish for lunch or dinner. It has an honorary place on the menu of every Viennese restaurant that's worth its salt.

"Fuck her!" After the first bite, Horsey forgot about Joy and his rival.

Instead, he admired the golden breadcrumb coating and… *Ahh…* and that juicy veal inner.

The schnitzel was served with warm potato salad: *Erdäpfel-salat*.

And all was washed down with Austrian beer.

Joy and that other guy were now completely forgotten—as if they had never existed. At least for the moment.

He was full and his mind empty. Horsey yawned. He felt tired. He asked for the bill but was told that Mr. Hubbell had picked up the check.

Hubbell who?

Horsey looked around. Joy was gone—and with her that nasty, disgusting, blatant, phony Hubbell.

Be that as it may. She'll come back.

Horsey drove home and went to sleep. Two hours later, Horsey woke up. He sat up in his bed. He heard a raspy voice. It wasn't Joy's.

"Listen. *Schnitzel, wann immer du dieses Wort hörst, sollten deine Antennen auf Empfang gestellt sein! When you eat one, you will be mine!!*"

Aha, the magic word was not *Shazam*! It was *Schnitzel!*

Whenever he heard **Schnitzel**, he was made to believe he would grow beyond himself. Finally, the whole nation would see a different Horsey. He was chosen to save the world and smash Communism.

Fortunately, he didn't have much to lose. A drop of blood, maybe, and a tiny piece of his brain but that could easily be spared in exchange for a good cutlet and the fame that would dazzle the woman of his dreams.

He was sure that great things may lie ahead of him.

Next day he received a phone call.

It was Mr. Distler. He was the friendliest in person.

There we go.

10 V-2 Over Distlerland

A GIANT CUCKOO CLOCK like that seen in the *Mousketeer Show* greeted the opening guests of Distlerland in general and its Futureland section in particular.

"Tomorrow can be a wonderful age," Walter Distler assured. "Our scientists today are opening the doors of the Space Age: to achievements that will benefit our children and generations to come. The Futureland attractions of this theme park have been designed to give you an opportunity to participate in adventures that are a living blueprint of our future." Distler promised "a vista into a world of wondrous ideas, signifying man's achievements... a step into the future, with predictions of constructive things to come. Tomorrow offers new frontiers in science, adventure, and ideals: the Atomic Age, the challenge of outer space, and the hope for a peaceful and unified world under the Stars and Stripes."

The event was broadcast nationwide. The MC passed the micro from Distler to America's premier rocket engineer, the man whose name was synonymous with innovation and future, with the journey through the impossible.

The engineer of the future was quite eloquent. He spoke, however, with a slight accent, a *German* accent but otherwise had changed his SS uniform for an American-style suit. He had

Americanized his manners and his name. Now he was Brown but still with "Von" in front. He even insisted that everybody should call him Von. Von and his assistants had provided the main attraction for the Futureland section: a huge V-2, like the ones he had built in Nazi Germany, missiles that were aimed at the stars—but sometimes hit London, as an English comedian once quipped.

Doris was cast to welcome him with flowers and a curtsy.

Horsey bowed when he handed Von the mike.

"Thank you, *Horsey*," said Von.

Horsey felt justifiably flattered. Didn't he hear correctly? Von Brown, this greatest scientist alive, knew his, knew Horsey's name!

Blessed are the poor in Spirit because theirs is the Kingdom of God. Ignorance is strength. Weakness of the mind connects your brain with those who have the power of thinking and monitoring.

We forgot to tell that Horsey was chosen to host the TV event. And he wasn't even asked to wear his large *Mousketeer* ears. Thanks to the magic *Schnitzel* pact, Horsey was on his way to become a major star. He was in an elated mood.

Von had smiled when he heard Distler talk about a peaceful world. He knew that, according to George Orwell, peace meant war: if not designed for peace, a space station could be a veritable weapon of destruction.

"*I appreciate your very welcome invitation, Horsey.*"

There was his name mentioned again. Horsey's breast swelled with pride.

"*And I would like to express my appreciation to Mr. Distler,*" Von continued his speech. "*He and I, we both are visionaries.*"

Horsey nodded. He was proud to have become part of the future game and one day even set foot on Mars. Joy should be extremely satisfied when he proposed to her. Hubbell will burst with envy.

"Once the United States will accept the challenge to apply its technology to my space aspirations, an all-out effort will follow. Here—and only here—is a new physical and scientific frontier, and its mysteries will capture the imagination of a pioneering people. Because of the fervor, determination, and the resources I am going to devote to space, this will be one of the finest periods in America's proud history. As space efforts slowly gain momentum over the years, one scientific and technological advance will follow the other, in rapid-fire order.

Today I take the opportunity, with Mr. Distler's friendly consent, to declare this Futureland and, with it, Space Age open."

Applause.

"While man's explorations were restricted to Earth, his spirit was constrained by a feeling of physical impossibility. In the future he will be free of this restraint, and more confident of his abilities.

War has been a catastrophe for mankind, no question about that, nobody will deny that, but—BUT war also advanced science at an incredible speed.

In April of 1937 our activities and personnel were transferred to Peenemünde on the Baltic. Five years later, in 1942, we had about completed the development of the V-2. Then we began concentrated development of the anti-aircraft guided missile 'Wasserfall', performing 44 successful launchings. The Peenemünde team had grown to 10,000 people by the end of World War II.

After the war, our dream continued. In the United States, at Fort Bliss in Texas, from September 1945 to April 1950, where we worked for the U.S. Army. About 120 handpicked members of the V-2 team were gradually supplemented by about 400 civilians and soldiers of the U.S. Army Ordnance Corps. Our first year here was a period of adjustment and professional frustration. Distrusted aliens in a desolate region of a foreign land, for the first time we had no assigned project, no real task. Nobody seemed to be much interested in work that smelled of weapons, now that the war was over. And space flight was a word border-

ing on the ridiculous. These lunatics dream of going to the Moon and—beyond.

In addition, to keeping our dream alive with V-2 evaluation firings at White Sands, New Mexico, we Germans began to study the American language, and the American way of life which we found superior to our previous life in Germany."

More applause.

"*Then, in April 1950, the army's rocket activities were transferred to Redstone Arsenal at Huntsville, Alabama, and when we crossed the Mississippi, things began to happen.*

It was here that I met Herr Distler for the first time. A mutual friend introduced us. He was raised in a rural town in Alabama. I liked him immediately. He was down to earth but not close-minded. No, he recognized that me and my men represented the future. He opened TV to us, and he opened his dream project of this theme park that bears his name to our vision.

Why—I ask you—why should a man who brought the best German fairy tales to the screen, the creator of Snow-White and Rose-Red *be an enemy of Germany, the man who brought King Ludwig's Neuschwanstein Castle to America?*"

Distler, as we know the walking incarnation of the dead King, was touched, moved to tears as his look fell on the silhouette of the impressive castle. Doris offered him a handkerchief.

Nobody noticed what happened in the meantime on the backlot of Futureland.

Mickey, the sponsor's naughty boy, watched some armed security guards chase a man who looked suspicious. The guards moved a little stiffly but they were fast. The stranger tried to hide somewhere, but Mickey had seen where he disappeared and pointed the guards in the right direction.

There was a brief shoot-out and the suspect dropped dead at the feet of a giant statue of Mortimer Mouse.

Mickey grinned.

The suspect was *Adolf Hitler*!

But why did Hitler have to die? Wasn't he already dead?

Distler thanked Von effusively for his speech. He almost kissed him like a party comrade but kept himself in check.

Von left the VIP stand accompanied by Horsey. There was Joy downstairs. She looked so beautiful.

Suddenly an inner voice told Horsey to kiss her in front of the cameras. Joy didn't object. They had told her.

To the Devil with Hitler! To the Devil with Hubbell!!

11 The Mystery of the Skull Ring

AT THE SAME TIME there was a family reunion. Some German people met to celebrate the confirmation of a teenage boy in the East of Germany, the German Democratic Republic, in a village not far away from Hoyerswerda in Saxony, a city with a history dating back to the early medieval ages and with the curtain open to the future. In 1928 Konrad Zuse, who later invented the world's first functional program-controlled Turing-complete computer, the Z3, passed his Abitur in Hoyerswerda. But besides all computer pioneering (and setting up a brown coal power plant named *Schwarze Pumpe* that would multiply the population by ten), they still told the fantastic yarn of the *Satanic Mill*, a Sorbian tale dealing with *Black Magic*. In this area they had very powerful means of keeping witches at bay which are the Walpurgis bonfires. Around Hoyerswerda they called these fires *"Burning the Witches"*: fires to rid the country of pestilence and vermin and with it destroy the evil spirit of Judas, the traitor, the incarnate Jew. In modern times, when witches were no more available as they were in the fairy tale mind of *Hansel and Gretel*, the unfulfilled German animation dream, they would burn books and a different breed of suspects to keep the folkloric tradition alive.

In almost every German family there were things nobody bothered to mention: deep, dark secrets, unsolved mysteries. You better kept your mouth shut. They considered it their human right to cast a veil of silence over unpleasant facts that would put the cute *garden gnome* mask from their grim visage. Stop asking questions.

Nobody would have mentioned "Uncle" Albin's presence that day. He was just there in East Germany to be with his godchild (who was named after a Norse God, by the way: Balder) although he was no East German. He was a *West* German. The Inner German border wasn't that closely guarded at that time. It was some years later when they found out that too many people were leaving the Eastern Zone and Walter Ulbricht, back then the State Party's strong man, his pointed beard an easy target for caricaturists, followed Chairman Mao's clever advice to build a wall after the pattern of the Chinese prototype to keep the West-German Fascists out and all others in.

Albin shouldn't have been there anyway. East German authorities were looking for guys like him to shove them in jail.

The family members kept their mouths shut about the unexpected visitor in a conspiracy of silence. Nobody knew that "Uncle" Albin would be coming. After a few drinks, however, the spell was broken—and being among like-minded persons, they would open the mouth and were bosom buddies unified in their hatred of the Communists.

"Uncle" Albin—which is not his real name, we have changed it, like others in this book (Albin in Germanic means: *protective friend*)—was a handsome man: tall and muscular, a chiseled, clean-shaven chin that wouldn't tolerate any dissent, a not too high forehead covered by blond hair. "Uncle" Albin was not so much a man of intellect, but a man of unbending will and loyalty who faintly looked like Paul Richter, the actor who starred as Siegfried the dragon slayer in a declared Nazi favorite, *Die Nibelungen* directed by Fritz Lang in the early 1920s, when Hitler made his first bid for power and attempted his unsuccessful Beer Hall Putsch in Munich.

Actually, "Uncle" Albin was proud that as a young Hitler Youth his fair head could be glimpsed in a movie too, Helen Bertha's Nazi epic *Triumph of the Will,* made at the Nuremberg Party Rally of 1934. Back then Albin had a close-up as drummer boy. Now he was to become a high-ranked soldier, a Lieutenant Colonel of the newly created West-German *Bundeswehr* and its tanks of Krupp steel, and therefore shouldn't have entered the Soviet Zone of Germany but he was no coward. Of course, he had crossed the border in plain clothes. He truly loved his nephew and—that's for sure: He loved the feeling to outmatch those primitive East-Germans and bedazzle them.

"Uncle" Albin had been a member of Hitler's *Wehrmacht* or, to be more precise: the *Waffen-SS.* As a man of war, he never had to change his identity like so many German compatriots who became known as wrynecks, persons of twisted identity.

As we said: on that day back in the late 1950s, the alcohol flowed freely. Beer bottle after beer bottle was opened. "Uncle" Albin didn't need a bottle opener, he used his plain teeth to remove the crown cap. He also didn't need to use the outside toilet, a privy, that often as the other males. Beer makes pee but Albin was hardboiled and overcame the temptation of nature.

Nevertheless, everybody pitied "Uncle" Albin who had suffered like Christ during World War II but remained unchanged and faithful to his people, race, and conviction.

The Russian campaign, he had to admit, was a *Sauerei*: a complete mess.

In only two days, on 5 and 6 December 1943, his unit, the so-called "Blowtorch Battalion", under the command of Lieutenant and SS Standartenführer Joachim Peiper—Jochen (as he called him)—had 2280 Soviet soldiers killed and took only three prisoners.

"He was a hard man, yes. We behaved like animals. We were no longer in control of ourselves. Women, children, entire villages…" Albin stammered when the children were to bed and innocent blood could be spilled, at least in memory.

Only the young confirmand boy, Balder, was permitted to stay. They thought that "Uncle" Albin's pithy words would help him to become a real man. "Say, Uncle Albin," the boy asked, "2280 Commies killed in only two days. That isn't bad, isn't it?"

A grateful "Uncle" Albin would stroke Balder's head occasionally while he continued to drink. "We understand each other, the boy and I. To us these Russian dogs were not human. We wanted to create a better humanity. But to rebuild one has to destroy inferiority first. Extinguish what is not worth living."

The ring on his finger gleamed. "We were drunk, all drunk. In our tanks we had the best French champagne…" Albin was a little disappointed that only beer would be served in East Germany now (this was worse than war), luckily with enough corn schnapps. "We were in a frenzy… blood frenzy… Children against door posts… the brain splashed and splattered."

Suddenly, the tough soldier cried uncontrollably. But he wasn't grieving about the victims they had killed and slaughtered in cold blood. No, the teary-eyed soldier only felt sorry for himself. Everybody at once tried to comfort and console the "poor man" who had suffered so much for the glory of Nazi Germany. The victims themselves they looked upon as "*Untermenschen*"— sub-humans. The clear objective of the Third Reich was to create precious Aryans and fight everything that was degenerated. To them, the war was a giant purgatory necessary to burn out the shame and disgrace of inferior races and cleanse the world.

Somehow Balder felt disgusted and strangely fascinated as well.

Finally, "Uncle" Albin recovered and literally rose from the dead. He was in agony and ecstasy at the same time. His mood had changed, his spirits rose, and again he became the proud peacock of yesteryear. Mentioned the medals they had received for their "deeds", recalling the *Führer Oath*, the feeling of being chosen. He recalled the formula of the *Hitlerjugend* and asked Balder to repeat it, word for word: "*In the presence of this blood banner, which represents our Führer, I swear to devote all my energies and my strength to the savior of our country, Adolf Hitler. I am willing and ready to give up my life for him, so help me God.*"—A common soldier would "*swear by God this holy oath, that I want to offer unconditional obedience to the Führer of the German Reich and people, Adolf Hitler, the commander-in-chief of the Wehrmacht, and be prepared as a brave soldier to risk my life for this oath at any time.*"—There were other, stronger oath formulas, like that of the fanatic 33rd Charlemagne soldiers: "*I swear to you, Adolf Hitler, Germanic Führer and Remaker of Europe, to be loyal and brave. I swear to obey you and the leaders you have placed over me until death.*"

In those days, heroes didn't look like effeminate pop stars. Their fingers were not in dope but in blood. The ring "Uncle" Albin wore on one of those fingers attracted not only Balder's interest. It seemed to be a *Totenkopfring*, a Skull Ring, ideally suited for anybody who would bring death.

"Say, Albin," one of the male guests asked. "Is this one of the famed Honor Rings of the SS?"

"Psst!" made "Uncle" Albin. "We don't talk about *that*. Talking too much could be a hanging matter. And anyway, it's only a replica."

They all laughed, "A replica?"

"Yes, the original I left in Hollywood."

Hollywood!

"You were... in Hollywood?!" The East Germans didn't trust their ears. The color of their faces changed from yellow to white.

But "Uncle" Albin seemed to be dead serious.

"I just returned from there. I was hired by the big studios as a consultant on war films."

He picked a photo out of his pocket. The picture showed him with British actor James Mason, both in accurate Nazi uniforms.

The reason for the existence of a production like *The Desert Fox* (1951) with James Mason in the title role of Field Marshal Erwin Rommel produced by Twentieth Century-Fox was Cold War which made the former enemy to an ally. Consequently, many German elite soldiers were turned into heroes, only misled by their Führer, but to no fault of their own. Now they were needed to build a new German army. (Originally, 20th-Fox intended to cast Kirk Douglas instead of Mason but then they followed Albin's advice to reject Kirk because he was Jewish and get Mason who looked more Aryan.)

From the Flaming Pages of a Great Best Seller...

From the Searing Sands of the Vast African Desert

Comes a Mighty Story With all the ADVENTURE the Screen Can Hold!

THE DESERT FOX

Africa: In the dark days when the storm of conflict turned the sand of a wasteland into a swirling fury.

Here one man whose daring became legend spread the saga of cunning and courage across the tugless wastes.

Sometimes the hunter, sometimes the hunted.

Always the wily commander known to friend and foe alike as THE DESERT FOX.

The Startling Story the World Has Only Guessed At...

Never Known Until Now!

Thrill-Thundering Adventure to Inflame Your Emotions!

Memorable Entertainment from 20th Century-Fox

(Rio, by the way, was used in that production as a light double for Adolf Hitler, played by another Jew, Luther Adler. "Uncle" Albin felt sorry for the Führer being portrayed by Jews but he wasn't going to sabotage the otherwise valuable production.)

Many errors have been made. Himmler had declared it himself shortly before he committed suicide. They all were somehow suicidal. On April 21, 1945, he said, "We have made horrible mistakes. If I could have a fresh start, I would do many things differently now. But it's too late now. We wanted greatness and security for Germany, and we are leaving behind us a pile of ruins, a fallen world..."

In 1946, for the sake of Himmler and the ghosts of the dead to whom he had sworn absolute loyalty, "Uncle" Albin had been in a death chamber himself for half a year being declared a war criminal. He and 74 of his comrades, mostly from the 1st SS Panzer Division "Leibstandarte Adolf Hitler", were on trial. Forty-six of them were finally sentenced to death by hanging, including Peiper and himself. "That was not fair. *That* thing occurred accidentally. It was nothing like the Russian campaign. I was innocent but waiting for death daily and not knowing why."

Because of some accidentally slaughtered American GIs he had clay feet now.

The so-called accident they were sentenced for was well documented: One of the meanest, most evil Nazi crimes that occurred during the *Battle of the Bulge* and concerned the Massacre of Malmédy on December 17, 1944. It was one of the worst (known) atrocities committed against prisoners of war in the West European sector during World War II.

They had encountered and fired on an American Battery:

"During an observation halt on the road from Thirimont to the northwest, about 800 to 1200 meters east of the Baugnez intersection, we saw an enemy truck column negotiating the intersection moving to the south," Albin recalled precisely. "The lead panzer element opened fire with high-explosive shells against the traveling column. Several vehicles immediately caught fire, the column became confused and vehicles began running off the road and into each other. The crews dismounted and sought over. We were hit by machinegun and rifle fire from the dismounted crews and had to defend ourselves. We returned the fire with our on-board machine guns and hastened our attack into the standing column. Eventually, the Americans stood up from the roadside ditch and raised their hands to surrender. What exactly happened afterwards I do not know. I guess the POWs wanted to flee, so they had to pass away. I learned later that they were shot when they tried to escape. *Auf der Flucht erschossen*, you know. That's how we called it in those days."

Shot when trying to escape.

But in the end, he, Albin, prevailed instead of becoming a martyr like those weak early Christians. The death penalty was not executed. "We cleared our names and became free men again. But we didn't want to be free. We wanted to follow our vocation and our oath serving the Fatherland as faithful soldier men."

Edeltraud, Albin's sister, assisted him with her eyes gleaming, "Do you know that the first word Albin said when he was a child was not *Papa* or *Mama*?"

Albin laughed recalling the memory.

"What was the first word?" the others were eager to know.

"*Data!*"

"*Data?*"

"That's short for *Sol-dat*, soldier."

Everybody in the circle roared with laughter. So, the one and only thing Albin aimed for right from the cradle was becoming a soldier.

To be more precise: At about 14:15, at Baugnez near Malmédy, soldiers from the 1st SS Panzer Division opened fire on the POWs. There are contradictory statements, but it is a fact that on December 12 Hitler had issued an order which stated that no prisoners were to be taken and that a "wave of terror" was to descend on the Allies who stood in the way of the offensive. Eighty-four POWs were *murdered*.

"I didn't shoot any of them. In this case I was completely innocent. The rest was done at the Führer's command. The oath, you know, was holy to us..."

Again, he wept some crocodile tears and wallowed in self-pity which he drowned in more alcohol.

"If Hitler would have won the war, things would have looked better," his sister said. "We all are victims of *Siegerjustiz* [victor's justice], you in the West and us in the East. Roosevelt, Truman, Churchill, Stalin—what does it matter?"

"But we all were valiant. All who served with me in my lead tank were valiant I can assure. They behaved like German soldiers, including the Tibetan who was the fastest gunner I've met in Sepp Dietrich's whole tank army."

"A—*Tibetan*? From Tibet?"

"Yeah, a born soldier. There was a good number of war volunteers from the Himalayas fighting on our side. Mostly they joined our Cossack regiments and our mountain troops. They were tough, you know, exceptional horsemen with endurance of sub-zero temperatures who refused to surrender. They fought to the last. The Tibetan was a true Aryan! The Reichsführer was very fond of him."

"Himmler?"

Albin nodded.

Himmler. This name brings us back to the ring. Albin allowed Balder to wear the replica: "You know, boy, Weisthor has designed that."

"Weisthor?"

"Well, Weisthor was not his real name. He was Karl Maria Wiligut. He was Austrian, you know. He was born in Vienna."

Wiligut-Weisthor was in fact one of the most bizarre characters in the Reichsführer's SS Camelot. Weisthor, or Thor, the wise warrior, became sort of Himmler's Rasputin. He blamed his wife's inability to conceive a healthy boy child on a Zionist-Masonic-Catholic conspiracy, which he also believed was responsible for the collapse of the Habsburg dynasty and his homeland's defeat in the war. After repeatedly threatening to kill his wife, he was confined to an asylum in Salzburg and diagnosed as a paranoid schizophrenic with megalomaniacal tendencies. On his release, he emigrated to Germany and in 1933 was introduced to the Reichsführer who had a soft spot for madmen.

Weisthor was not only instrumental in designing the SS uniform and the Death's Head Ring which bore his family seal but in the purchase of Wewelsburg and its restoration into an SS Order castle under the Black Sun, with a concentration camp within shouting distance in Niederhagen. Once the castle had been the seat of the 16th century bishops and witch-hunters of Paderborn. Its round table and ritual chamber in the basement of the north-facing tower were intended to become both the headquarters of Himmler's nascent warrior knight dynasty and the geographic center of a new World Order.

Wewelsburg became the Camelot of the SS, located not far from Teutoburg forest, where Teutonic hero Arminius had defeated the legions of the Roman occupants under General Varus.

Albin had been there on Wewelsburg to pledge undying allegiance to Hitler and SS Germany.

"We believe in Adolf Hitler,
the immortal Leader of our race,
singular gift of Providence,
greatest figure of all time,
alive in our hearts today and forever.

We believe in his Holy Cause,
Which is the New Order,
the fulfillment of Aryan destiny
in accordance with the eternal laws of life,
the hope and future of our kind on earth.

We believe in his Movement,
the true, undivided body of his followers,
which bears the name of his Cause

as the instrument of his will,
consecrated by the blood of heroes and martyrs
- *the only way to world redemption.*
HEIL HITLER!"

Albin's expression transfigured. To him it was like yesterday and the oath still valid.

Weisthor himself had handed them their Death Head's Rings. He got one—and the Tibetan too.

"Gee, one day I like to go there," Balder exclaimed. "I like to go on a pilgrimage to Wewelsburg. I like to fight like you, Uncle Albin, and the Tibetan."

Again, Albin stroked the boy's head, "Not flesh and blood have revealed this to you, my boy. There are many enemies in Asia, Balder. More than a billion. But Tibet is our protection shield, a staging post between Mongol and European races, with the European racial roots strongly manifested in Tibetan aristocracy. They are our brothers. I know. They fought on our side. There are old legends that tell that Aryans, led by Thor himself, once fled a cataclysm to settle in Tibet. Many Tibetans therefore have German roots. The Tibetan was my blood brother."

Weisthor, for instance, claimed that the Bible had originally been written in Germanic, and testified to an "Irminic" religion— Irminen religion or Irminism that contrasted with Wotanism. He claimed to worship a Germanic God "Krist", whom Christianity was supposed later to have appropriated as their own savior Christ. According to Weisthor's gospel, the original Christ never ever was a Jew. Krist dated back to 12,500 BC. Germanic culture and history reached back to 228,000 BC. At that time, there was not one, there were *three* suns, and Earth was inhabited by giants, dwarfs, and other mythical creatures.

Albin was still in awe when he talked about Wiligut: "Weisthor developed his own rune row that consisted of 24 letters: Tel, Man, Kaun, Fa, Asa, Os, Eis, Not, Tor, Tyr, Laf,

Rit, Thorn, Ur, Sig, Zil, Yr, Hag-Al, H, Wend-horn, Gibor, Eh, Othil, Bar-Bjork."

What he didn't mention was that, like many of his compatriots, Weisthor didn't look Aryan at all. He was a dumpy character with stubby, glassy eyes and a bottle nose. But while in jim-jams, he dreamed of a New World Order.

Karl Maria Wiligut a.k.a. Weisthor had died on January 3, 1946. His madness, however, was still alive now that Albin had passed his original death-bringing ring to a brain trust in Hollywood that worshipped it as a relic.

"It now can be seen in a shrine at Neuschwanstein Castle in Distlerland. You know, Distler is our man!!"

"Gee, Distlerland, Uncle Albin," Balder rejoiced. "Wish I could go there one day."

Albin looked squarely into Balder's eyes: "You keep it. You will keep and cherish my replica ring, Balder. It will open the gates of Disterland. One day. And don't forget your Uncle Albin. And don't forget our Führer. Promise?"

"Scout's honor!"

But back to the *Desert Fox*. For that particular movie, thanks to Albin's intervention, America refrained from the usual Hollywood pattern of the arrogant German general. In this Rommel picture all German generals were portrayed sympathetically, with the only exception of Wilhelm Keitel, who according to reality didn't appear as militarist but as Hitler's minion.

In the movie, Rommel is disgusted by Hitler's command that his armies seek "victory or death". Gradually, he turns against the Führer. Rommel's opposition to Hitler has helped create his image as the Second World War German field marshal it's okay to like. Though he fought for Hitler, he never joined the Nazi party. On the other hand, he did fight for Hitler—and admired him. Because the film focuses on the last few months of Rommel's life, it shows much more of Rommel doubting Hitler than loyally serving him—a balance some felt had been pushed too far. When *The Desert Fox* came out, it was slammed in the *New York Times* as "a tenderised Hollywood laudation" of "the leader responsible for the deaths of thousands upon thousands of British troops, the crafty general so righteously hated as the dragoman of Hitler".

Joy and her fiancé Horsey had attended the premiere and loved the movie. Soon after they were married and still in love—although Horsey harbored the suspicion that she was still in touch with Hubbell. For any eventuality. Better keep an eye on her!

12 The Donkeys of Pleasure Island

IT CAME AS A SURPRISE to Horsey that Von had personally selected him to be the host of his next, most ambitious TV show on Distler TV. *The Conquest of the Universe (and Beyond)* was a mix of Distler animation and live action with Von and his team interviewed by Horsey.

To the public, Von presented himself a technically highly gifted dreamer. Thanks to Distler's show and with the popular Horsey supporting him as submissive sycophant, he reached and fascinated an audience of millions. Amidst a technological race of systems with the Soviet Union, Von ingeniously transformed into an agent of an allegedly non-political dream of mankind: to set foot on the Moon—but that was to be not the end, only the beginning. Mars was high on Von's agenda too. That was music to Horsey's ears.

"Is there life on Mars?"

Von nodded, "I am sure."

"Intelligent life?"

"We'll see."

The new program was hot and influential in captivating the attention of the public, igniting the imagination of viewers, and shaping the culture with a desire and dream of space exploration.

Von's shows (as presented by Horsey) were considered essential in moving the space program forward and were historic in their significance.

In private, Von remained a man of WW2. In spring 1940, an emissary from Heinrich Himmler had arrived in Peenemünde and handed Von an invitation by the Reichsführer to become a member of the SS. The SS was keen on having a hand in every secret technology.

In the final days of the Third Reich, one of Von's friends, Albert Speer, was said to have had the idea of killing Hitler with poison gas. Nothing happened, however, but the say-so helped Speer to escape the gallows in Nuremberg. Von did something similar to redeem himself in the eyes of the victors. He claimed to have tried some resistance against the regime. He said that he had been arrested 2:00 a.m. in the morning of March 22, 1944, one day before his birthday, because he had suggested, under the influence of alcohol, that the rockets they built were meant to support the idea of space travel, not national defense. Of course, Von was released immediately as Hitler needed him to bomb London with rocket speed but that didn't matter. He was able to make Americans believe that he was in opposition to the Nazis. So, after war was over, Von never was to make the acquaintance of the executioner. Instead, thanks to Project Paperclip, he made himself comfortable and a well-paid career on Sauerkraut Hill in the United States. Paperclip was a secret U.S. intelligence program that brought German scientists, engineers, and technicians in great numbers to America. President Truman had authorized Paperclip personally to exploit those German scientists for U.S. research, and to deny these intellectual resources to the Soviet Union. Some reports bluntly pointed out that these people were "ardent Nazis". But they were considered so vital to Cold War effort that they were invited over to the States: more than 1,600 of them! Some of these experts had even participated in murderous medical experiments on human subjects such as Dr. Ziska and Dr. Todt but the necessities of Cold War turned yesterday's enemies into today's allies. CIA personnel were not opposed to working with Nazi doctors and scientists who had proven to be proficient in breaking the mind and rebuilding it: *staatskonform*—in a way consistent with state interests. It was decided that the alleged Communist threat was an issue that took priority over constitutional rights.

The timing was great. Von and his colleagues benefitted from Cold War. Determinedly, Von became an advocate of the intensification of the arms race in the 1950s and spoke up publicly for a policy of strength, even for a preemptive strike against the Soviet Union. It was the blueprint of SDI, the Strategic Defensive Initiative. Von's ideas emanated almost one-on-one from his youth fantasy Lunetta: an artificial Earth's moon shaped as a wheel armed with atomic weapons orbiting the planet as "decisive weapon" and thus enforcing world peace.

If a moron like Hubbell was going to influence the human subconscious mind with a makeshift idiot box, Von's technical flights of fancy and pipe dreams superseded him by light-years. And Horsey was justifiably proud to be part of those light-years ahead. He felt like Moses leading his people into the promised land of the future. All the universe or nothing, he said with Raymond Massey, the star of H. G. Wells' 1936 movie *Things to Come*.

Conquest of the Universe (and Beyond) was so successful that President Dwight D. Eisenhower asked Distler for a print to show it to his generals. Ike was under pressure. The Soviets were in space already. They had launched Sputnik-1 which many Americans were made to believe a second Pearl Harbor. Before Sputnik, Eisenhower's popularity was up to 79%, after Sputnik it sank to 57%. One has to imagine: a TV show made for the minds of 12-year-olds and then it was used by the military! As a consequence, NASA was established. Von was promoted to become the spiritual Columbus of Space Age. He moved on to suggest to the new President, John F. Kennedy, that America had a good chance to win the race and triumph over Russia. East German

Staatssicherheit (Stasi) tried to scatter some sand into the gearbox and published a book about Von's SS membership, but at the peak of Cold War it didn't do any harm.

Although the American public was skeptical towards the billions of tax money the space age would devour, the attitude changed when Horsey's Von show was broadcast. The project helped Von and it helped the goals of the Distler masterminds who wanted not only to conquer the universe but, in a roundabout way, the human brain.

Within seconds of watching Horsey's show on TV, they had found out, people's minds would slip into a hypnotic trance state. It lowered the brainwaves to a lower 'alpha state' commonly associated with meditation and deep relaxation. This was believed to be caused by the screen flicker and explained why one felt sleepy while watching Distler TV. The subconscious mind, which carried all memories and beliefs, was directly programmed by watching TV. It became highly suggestible and whatever information you were going to receive from TV, right or wrong, intelligent or absurd, were to become part of your memory pool. Since beliefs were nothing but memories, this information had the tendency to alter beliefs or form new ones when it seeped into one's subconscious mind. You might have thought the remote was in your hand and you're the one who decides watching what programs but, in truth, *you* were the one who is getting programmed.

That was how Horsey himself met Dr. Tristan Todt for the first time. Todt was the alchemist behind Humor's creations and the father of Doris. Dr. Todt was polite to no end when Horsey showed up and declared him the coming man. Horsey modestly waved off but felt flattered and cajoled.

Todt told him that Distler wanted to make him not only the host of Von's shows but an associate producer too.

Horsey could hardly believe his luck.

"There's only a slight condition."

"?"

Todt who wore meticulously polished, squeaking leather boots led Horsey to a black box and opened it.

Inside was something swimming in a nutrient. It looked like a—

"*Schnitzel?*"

"Not exactly. Sure, it's flat. But it's a brain."

"A brain? The brain of an animal?"

Todt looked at him in disgust, "Of course not! It's human!! In fact, it's *über*menschlich!!!"

"Ubermenshlick?"

"Ja, superhuman. The greatest brain that ever lived—and is still alive. This brain is immortal. And now we are going to connect you with its brainwaves."

"Connect … me … with the greatest brain ever? But it will hurt."

"Don't be afraid. We are experts in this technique. There will be no pain. You will volunteer as *Schnittstelle* between this very brain and our audience."

"???"

"The interface. You will link them. Live. On TV."

"What I am going to tell them…?"

"Don't panic. Just sit down and relax. You will know when you wake up…"

Todt motioned an assistant who brought a cable. Plugs were fastened on Horsey's neck. For a moment he looked like Boris Karloff's Frankenstein monster.

Horsey saw the Schnitzel brain glow and pulsate like *Donovan's Brain*, the undying beast from German émigré writer Curt Siodmak's horror novel: A scientist discovers that a human brain can survive death and destruction and continue to function as a dynamo of living thought generating a mental power greater than the science of man.

Horsey felt a high voltage shock, electrifying in its thrilling intensity. Then he fell into the arms of Morpheus and began to snore.

He had wild dreams.

He saw a coach. Inside the coach were noisy kids. A fat, feisty coachman swinging his horse whip brought them with an evil grin to a theme park. The coachman was Breezy. The lead horse, by the way, was Crash. Crash grinned too.

The park they entered looked like Distlerland!

It was like Carlo Collodi's immortal tale of *Le avventure di Pinocchio* that was published in 1881 in an Italian children's magazine and transformed into an animated feature film by Distler some 50 years later. There was a chapter that told of children being lured by a ruthless Coachman to *Paese dei balocchi*, the Land of Toys or Pleasure Island with the promise of having fun all time but when they arrived, they were turned into *donkeys*! The donkeys then were sold to farms, salt mines and circuses.

At the end, high above Distlerland, on the Tower of Distler's Neuschwanstein replica, a flag was hoisted. The flag was red, with a white circle, and inside the circle was a black swastika.

Horsey's mouth was dry when he woke up, "What are *we* going to do with the donkeys, Herr Todt?"

"Speak German! *Sprechen Sie Deutsch!!*"

"Aber ich kann doch nicht Deutsch..."

"Sie können sehr wohl, Horsey!"

"Deutsch... Ich... spreche... die... Sprache... von Goethe.... und Schiller."

Yes, now Horsey spoke the language of Johann Wolfgang von Goethe and Friedrich Schiller, the great German poets... the language of Goethe's Faust, the alchemist who signed a pact with the devil, and the language of Adolf Hitler who led the guileless, pleasure-seeking donkeys to death and destruction!

Now Horsey had been transformed into a Junior Devil. He had received the baptism of fire—with the prospect of being promoted to America's Chief Devil one day. It would last—but the conspirators from Hell had time.

Eile mit Weile! One step at a time!!

Horsey felt for his ears. They were normal. No donkey ears. Horsey was relieved. But wait a moment... Hey, there were horns on his head. He looked for a mirror and saw two horns growing out of his head, like Pinocchio's nose, long and longer.

Scared to death he woke up a second time.

No Dr. Todt around. He was in his bedroom. Joy was half asleep.

"Joy, I got horns. Like the devil."

Joy rubbed her eyes and looked: "Nonsense, Horsey. Go to sleep. I'm tired. I have to get up early for another day of shooting."

"Shooting? What movie?"

"*Donovan's Brain*! An interesting story about an undying brain... Imagine, I got 10... *ten* pages of dialogue!"

She took a screenplay from her nightstand and began to read:

That man... he was dying, but his brain was still alive. It was an extraordinary brain, the dome large and of perfect shape, the skull broad, the forehead wide. We have to keep it alive! Under any circumstances!

Blob!

13 Inside Hitler's Brain

HORSEY ENJOYED his newly-won power as associate producer. To prove it to himself he asked his office to contact Breezy and sign him as director. Now there was his chance to take revenge on that man and punish and torment him and make him a fool in front of a TV crew.

Breezy was currently unemployed and desperately needed a job. He had gone too far and caused an accident which delayed production and cost money. This time Hollywood didn't take it easy. He was banned from movie sets.

"This man," Horsey said while introducing Breezy to the crew, "this man is the living proof how low one can stoop if he ignores true talent." True talent—that was him. And Breezy was to become his whipping boy, "In the future you will be paid to kiss my ass. And if you don't, you will end up in the gutter where you belong to. Believe me, I will give you ulcers."

While Horsey was engaged in his personal vendetta, Tristan Todt, the alchemist, brain surgeon and inventor, and Distler's henchmen were busy conducting further experiments about human brainwaves and television. They found that in less than one minute of television viewing, human brainwaves switched from Beta waves—brainwaves associated with active, logical thought—

to primarily Alpha waves. The Alpha state is a relaxed state of mind that feels really peaceful. The more we watch TV, the more the state continues and—increases.

Brain activity would switch from the left to the right hemisphere. The right brain treated incoming data uncritically, processing information in wholes, leading to emotional, rather than logical responses. The pleasurable feeling while watching TV could become quite addictive and transform the viewer into a 'couch potato'. The shift from left to right brain activity caused the release of endorphins, the body's own natural opiates. Thus, it was likely to become physically addicted to watching TV and get a mere tool.

The Alpha brainwave state makes us more susceptible to what we are watching. It leaves us feeling receptive to what we are viewing. It is like a hypnotic state where we are suggestible to whatever is being shown, be it news or political propaganda. Activity in the higher brain regions is diminished, while the lower brain regions, the reptile brain, respond. To the reptile brain, if it looks real, it is real. Though we know on a conscious level it is "only a movie" or entertainment, on the other level we do not. The heart will beat faster, while we watch a suspenseful or horrific scene. The reptile brain makes it possible for us to survive as biological beings, but it also leaves us vulnerable to the image manipulations of TV that often remain undetected. This way, the brain is gradually conditioned. Even if they tell you that you are a Schnitzel, you will believe it.

Not you but the images and messages televised or digitized are the ones that obsess you. Following Doctor Todt's experiments with TV imagery, hundreds of thousands of hidden images and blunt sales messages were transmitted to the brains of American citizens.

Von's Distlerland TV show became an ideal test ground.

Two years later the dark forces behind him began to mount a political campaign that was supposed to catapult Horsey right into the political headquarters, make him at least Governor of California and after that… well, time would decide.

Unfortunately, for Horsey that meant a return to horses. The organization knew that Horsey once was a minor cowboy star and so he should be back in the saddle. They were sure that animal love would help him win the election. Particularly women love horses—and so women voters will love Horsey.

There was no resistance on Horsey's part.

"You will do what they tell you," Joy demanded while she browsed through the pages of a fashion magazine. "And if they ask you to settle with the penguins at North Pole you will do too."

"Penguins on North Pole? I thought they're at South Pole."

"Don't be that pedantic, will you. I don't care. Just do what they expect of you."

Horsey made a distrustful face but laughed it off in front of the camera. Luckily, he had his whipping boy, Breezy, acting as his perennial laughing stock.

Say about him what you want, but a real pro and trooper Horsey was. And don't forget the magic spell of *Schnitzel* which worked wonders.

The shooting with Horsey and his old enemy Crash (a.k.a. "Breezy's Revenge") didn't proceed smoothly. Horsey needed many takes and was thrown out of the saddle in each. Finally, they had to turn to a stunt double. Close-ups with Horsey were made back at the studio. Horsey sat on a mechanical horse in front of a background screen onto which a giant moon was projected. It looked as if Horsey, singing a song, would ride into the moonlight.

The song went something like this:
One n-i-i-i-i-g-h-t we will be up t-h-e-e-e-r-e
Up t-h-e-e-e-e-e-r-e on the M-o-o-o-o-o-o-o-n.

Horsey, however, insisted to exchange Moon for Mars because: "God speaks from the Red Planet."

To soothe him they shot an alternative version but made sure that Mars ended on the cutting room floor. Moon was in the script approved by the Organization and Moon was it.

But God would have to have his place too: "We can use the Old man." Therefore, the campaign saw Horsey also on the pulpit.

On selected Sundays, when enough cameras were around, he volunteered as minister in his local church (with as many reporters and photographers around as possible) where his sounding voice read the sermon to an overly pious community:

And the chief priests and scribes sought how they might kill HIM. And with them Satan entered into Judas surnamed Iscariot, being of the number of the twelve. And he went his way, and communed with the chief priests and captains, how he might betray him unto them. And they were glad, and covenanted to give him money. And he promised, and sought opportunity to betray him unto them in the absence of the multitude.

Horsey looked onto the community of his devout listeners:

These people, with Satan in their mind, tell Judas that they are going to give him money: Twelve ... twelve pieces of silver. This is probably why the word of God tells us that the root of all evilness is MONEY.

But all of a sudden, Horsey's throat became dry, and the godly words got stuck in the neck.

There, sitting in last row, was HITLER... no, not Hitler, more like Hitler's impersonator. There was RIO wearing Hitler's toothbrush mustache.

Horsey couldn't believe his eyes. He hadn't seen this man for years.

Confused, he interrupted his preaching and asked clearly audible, "Why... Why did you come here? What do you want from me?"

The members of the churchgoing community looked at each other: bewildered.

Horsey left the pulpit and walked down towards the phantom.

There he was in person: Rio, the man whose life he had sold to the devil for money and a career in media and politics.

Yes, *he*, Horsey, was the one who had given him, some ten years ago, the invitation to the opening of Distlerland to stylize himself as a hero, a hero that he never was. He had betrayed his friend and delivered Rio to the knife.

Rio had told him that he got scruples to continue in his TV part as Adolf Hitler.

"Why?"

"I'm not Rio," he had yelled.

"You aren't?"

"No, I am LIOR. LIOR VERDAH!! This is my Hebrew name. And the Nazis killed all my relatives."

"Come on! Stop talking trash! You aren't Jewish! Who told you so? Hitler wasn't a Jew! That Hitler guy was your acting coach! People loved your Hitler imitation."

"Yeah, I thought he was good for my acting! In fact, that TV part began to destroy my spirit. I realized that I was going to sell my soul to the devil. Like Faust did."

"Faust who? Say, are you a Commie? Don't you love the Germans? They are our allies now."

"Me? Not love the Germans?! Why shouldn't I love the Germans? 'Cause they are arrogant and bull-necked and do whatever they are ordered to if it's only gruesome? 'Cause they killed millions of Jews, people like me, in their concentration camps and made soap out of them and lamp shades for their houses? Is there any reason to hate these sumbitches?!"

Rio who was Lior had to tell it ALL. In the meantime, he said, he had learned that his relatives were killed near the end of the war in a German concentration camp located near Nordhausen in Thuringia, not far from the southern Harz Mountains, *Dora-Mittelbau.*"

"They should have loved and obeyed their Führer. Then they would have been spared this fate."

Lior Verdah shook his head.

Dora, so the codename, was founded in the summer of 1943 as a sub-camp of Buchenwald concentration camp, one of 88 sub-camps, when (after severe British bombing) the rocket production activities carried out at Peenemünde were relocated to tunnel facilities in Thuringia. Between 1943 and 1945, some 60,000 persons from nearly all European countries were deported to the Harz Mountains as concentration camp inmates to perform forced labor and assemble the parts for the Nazis' A-4 ballistic missiles, later christened the V-2 missile program, and other experimental weapons, the so-called *Vergeltungswaffen* (Weapons of Retaliation, Vengeance Weapons), in underground factories. One in three of the concentration camp inmates died.

"And do you know who was responsible?"

"Herr Hitler?"

"Yes, Herr Hitler! And your friend **Von**!!"

Von himself had claimed once and again that he never saw a single corpse at Dora, but Rio/Lior knew that he lied.

Rio/Lior had met one of the GIs who liberated that concentration camp and entered the hell of the underground factories of Mittelbau. That is what he said:

"You must realize that the American troops had no inkling, not even a rumor, of the grisly discovery that they were about to make… We were totally unprepared for what assaulted our senses or for the abruptness with which a new role was foisted on us. The half-crazed, emaciated victims trapped inside the camp barely resembled humans. Those who could walk, having heard the rumble of our tanks, had pressed themselves on the fence, crying, arms outstretched to their liberators. Some were too weak from starvation to even survive the emotion that enveloped prisoner and soldier alike."

Mittelbau (Central Construction) officially came into being on October 28, 1944, as part of the Dora network that by then operated almost entirely independent from Buchenwald. In charge of the operation on behalf of the SS was Brigadeführer Dr.-Ing. Hans Kammler. Camp commandant was SS-Sturmbannführer Otto Förschner. While the tunnels were being built, the unfortunate inmates of Dora were forced to sleep and live underground, in some cases not seeing the daylight for many months.

Early arrivals from Buchenwald lived in tents near the entrance to main tunnel B, but by the end of September 1943 the ever-growing number of prisoners were bedded on straw on the bare rock of cross-tunnel 39 until wooden bunks four levels high were built into dead-end tunnels 43 to 46 at the south end of main tunnel A. The dust, noise, and noxious gasses from the blasting and from trains hauling rock exacerbated an already catastrophic health situation for the concentration camp slaves. Water was in short supply. The only toilets were oil barrels cut in half with boards over them, but they were too few in number. Many of the unfortunates relieved themselves in the tunnels. The stench became intolerable, and disease and vermin proliferated. Soon, cases of pneumonia, tuberculosis, typhoid, and dysentery took a dreadful toll, combined with total exhaustion inflicted by 12-hour days of backbreaking labor.

By the end of January 1944 there were 12,682 prisoners registered. Eight to ten thousand of them lived underground like the Morlocks from H.G. Wells' *The Time Machine*. Morlock sounds a lot like Moloch, the name of the cruel Phoenician god associated with child sacrifice in the Bible. Since then, their Nazi tormentors preferred to work in the blackness of the underground to hide their Moloch-worthy crimes. Maybe Moloch himself would have been shocked. V-2 production started slowly, hampered by sabotage (more than 200 prisoners were hanged accused of sabotage), but with the arrival of better weather and the evacuation of the slaves from the tunnels into the barracks camp, the situation "improved".

Rio's relatives were among those accused of sabotage and hanged without trial.

A decade later, Lior called Rio finally saw a chance to sabotage Von's work: destroy this man's reputation on the lot of Distler's Futureland, not to assassinate Von, only to take a stand against Nazism and discredit the rocketeer in public.

Lior felt free since he disowned the Hitler part. He felt like himself again, had found back his lost identity, buried in the vaults of TV's entertainment industry.

Hearing all this from Rio's, no: Lior's mouth, Horsey went and communed with Distler's security who went forth and killed the poor Jew, like his relatives were killed: not beneath a statue of Adolf Hitler but beneath Distlerland's huge, shining symbol, Mortimer Mouse.

In his pocket they discovered a farewell letter. It led the guards to check the V-2. They found enough explosive to blow the rocket to smithereens but they diffused it in time and disposed of the "human waste" that once was Lior.

Nobody got wind of what had happened behind the curtain—and who was the traitor.

Then, like a ghost, Rio was gone. Horsey could finish his sermon and professed to God, Distler and his friend Von:

"By the grace of God, Von will take us to Mars."

14 Götterdämm-erung

BENEATH THE FAÇADE of German supermen glory was the Nazis' paradoxical obsession with death, ruin, and martyrdom. Inspired by Richard Wagner and the religion of Bayreuth, neo-Romanticism, monumentality of the banal, and *volkish* ideology, Hitler had crafted a Germany that was built on sacrifice, hero worship and—**Tod**: Death. The Nazi *Totenkult*, their Death Cult, had ended in national suicide and widespread immolation at the end of World War II: *Twilight of the Gods*—Wagner's *Götterdämmerung*.

Before she is consumed by flames, Brunhilde in Wagner's *The Ring of the Nibelung* cries out: *"Laughing let us be destroyed; laughing let us perish...let night descend, the night of annihilation...laughing death...laughing death."*

Hitler's religion hailed "The Cult of the Fallen Soldier", the Myth of Langemark. At Langemark, Belgium on 26th of October 1914, hundreds of young German soldiers marched into no man's land to their death while singing the opening verse of the *Deutschlandlied*, the Song of Germany:

Deutschland, Deutschland über alles, über alles in der Welt.—

Germany, Germany above all, above all in the world.

Thousands of young men were slaughtered, and the myths surrounding their death became the cornerstone of Nazism: *We are Germans; we fight for our people and shed our blood and hope that the survivors are worthy of our sacrifice. And if we go to our deaths with the hope for a purified, honorable Germany in our hearts, perhaps it is better than to have the victory. The struggle of mankind must continue in Eternity, Amen. No end to war!!!*

During the days of the Third Reich, the regime routinely peddled the notion that fallen Nazi comrades were not truly dead, but continued the fight for Germany as part of an immortal, spiritual army. This was important ideological glue for establishing the idea of People's Community: the *Volksgemeinschaft*.

Speaking at the anniversary of the 1923 Munich Bierhallen Putsch, in which 16 Nazis had been killed, Hitler declared in 1942:

Truly these sixteen who fell have celebrated a resurrection unique in world history... From their sacrifice came Germany's unity, the victory of a movement, of an idea and the devotion of the entire people... All the subsequent blood sacrifices were inspired by the sacrifice of these first men. Therefore, we raise them out of the darkness of forgetfulness and make them the center of attention of the German people forever. For us they are NOT DEAD. This temple is no crypt but an eternal watch. Here they lie as true martyrs of our movement.

Similarly, the fate of several members of the Nazi leadership after 1945 came to be mythologized, with various conspiracy theories questioning the cause, or very fact, of their deaths. Like Flying Saucers, the dead resurrected and were supposed to be seen across the world.

The passage of time had done little to diminish the Sympathy with the Devil, nor stem speculation surrounding the circumstances of his demise. Indeed, many people have doubted if Hitler died in his underground vault in Berlin at all. Survival myths remain popular fodder for tabloid newspaper articles, sensationalist TV documentaries, and best-selling books. In July 1945, *The Times* acknowledged that:

Whatever pronouncement is made, it is certain that many people in Germany, especially here in Berlin, will go on believing in the legend of his escape under cover of one of the doubles he is supposed to have employed.

The reporter of the *Daily Herald* concurred, noting, *no one with whom I have talked in Berlin believes that Hitler is dead. They all think he "got away".*

Got away—like a specter, like a phantom. One of these odd stories reveals that Hitler (after he had shaved) and his wife Eva made their escape through a network of bunkers beneath battle-torn Berlin. They resurfaced at a boulevard which had been turned into a makeshift runway. Here, a Luftwaffe pilot by the name of Captain Peter Baumgart frantically flew the Führer and his bride to Denmark from where the couple fled to Spain. Baumgart had been sentenced by a tribunal of three Polish judges to imprisonment for five years for being a member of the SS. Baumgart had told the tribunal that he was born in South-West Africa, but renounced British citizenship in 1935. He claimed he had shot down 128 Allied aircraft in Crete, Italy, North Africa and the Eastern Front, and was the holder of the Iron Cross and other decorations. He added that on May 25, 1945, shortly before the fall of Berlin, Hitler suddenly summoned him and ordered him to fly to Denmark. Hitler, Eva Hitler née Braun and a German general, with some others, boarded his plane in Berlin, and it took off for Denmark. The plane made a forced landing at Magdeburg, but, upon Hitler's insistence, he flew the following day through an artillery barrage to the Danish shore. They landed about 44 miles from the Eiter River in a field. Hitler shook hands with him, gave him a cheque for 20,000 marks, and ordered him to return to Berlin immediately.

From Denmark the party escaped to Spain. There, with fellow dictator Franco's aid, Herr and Frau Hitler took a submarine trip across the Atlantic to Argentina. Numerous eyewitness reports claimed that Hitler was spotted in Argentina for years after the war, in locations ranging from restaurants to hotels to hospitals.

Involuntarily, Horsey sympathized with the weird idea that Hitler could have resurrected from the dead and, via Argentina, came to California. Wouldn't it be better if Hitler played himself instead of Charlie Chaplin or Rio?!

Horsey's breast filled with pride given the thought that he was selected not by a cartoon producer like Distler but by the Führer himself who had chosen him for the post of Governor of California (and maybe more).

Yes, women loved Horsey's Horse Campaign and decided to ballot for him.

To Horsey, *Schnitzel* was Hitler and Hitler was inside his brain… But why would a declared vegetarian like Hitler name himself after a cutlet? Anyway, the voice had told him that it had more in mind for Horsey, even more in mind than Horsey, and that Joy's ambition would be fulfilled: to become First Lady of more than just California.

15 Hubbell in the Shoes of the Fisherman

JOY AND HORSEY were now a firm part of California's political elite. At home Joy called the tune. Joy, of course, had ambitions of her own. She was in touch with a female astrologer who was close to Hubbell, the man under whose spell she was, the man she loved dearly.

Although the conspirators, Hubbell's as well as Distler's, operated by similar means, they all were competing for the same popular Hollywood scalps. Thanks to Joy, Hubbell learned about Distler's secret plans and whereabouts. He was going to decide the leadership contest of winning most of Hollywood's and America's idiots for himself by kidnapping Old Man Distler and then blackmail Distler's Organization.

Day and location of the crime were set: April 30, Distler's private apartments (unknown to the public) high above Distlerland in the Tower of the Neuschwanstein replica. The plan worked. Distler put up no resistance. It was childishly simple.

But when Hubbell tried to interrogate him, Distler spluttered only digits.

"Okay then, take his scalp!" Hubbell demanded.

Distler showed no sign of fear or emotion when one of Hubbell's henchmen took a long knife.

"Damn, will you talk, son of a bitch!"

Distler shook his head, then pushed a button and opened it. Opened his brain.

"What's that? His brain is full of cables."

Hubbell began to understand, "He's a rowboat."

"A … row… boat?"

"Yeah, a mechanical man. A rowboat."

That's it: Distler was a *robot*. (Forgive Hubbell's peculiar pronunciation.)

Since his untimely death from smoking so much, there were several Distler duplicates around. The Organization itself was run by different forces. Distler and his duplicates had just become fronts.

As Hubbell knew the truth, the Distler Organization suggested to avoid confrontation and stake their claim: "Ours will be the minds, yours will be souls."

Hubbell thought it over and agreed. He took the money he was offered—but then was at a loss. How to hunt souls and catch them?

Maybe Joy would know. After all, she was a sensitive woman.

He found Joy in bed reading while Horsey was out on official duties. This time it was no women's magazine as usual. It was a book written by one Morris L. West. Joy handed Hubbell the copy. Hubbell read the title: *The Shoes of the Fisherman*. He had no idea what the book was about. He took his clothes off and joined her.

"It's about a new pope."

"Some papist stuff, eh?"

"When the Italian pope dies in the latter part of the twentieth century, the Cardinals debate who is going to succeed him."

"They usually do."

"But this time they elect a…"

"A… what? A rowboat?"

"Not exactly. The new pope is the youngest cardinal of them all—and a Russian."

"A Russian? Then he *is* a rowboat."

"In that conclave they elect a cardinal from Ukraine who reluctantly steps out from behind the Iron Curtain and tears down the wall. It's him who ends Cold War: Pope Kiril I. It's the future of politics: We are going to beat the most dangerous enemy of mankind, Communism, by the grace of God and turn everything into religion."

"Turn everything into religion? Hmm..."

"I tell you: The way to make a million dollars is to start a religion."

"You think I should open a Church?"

"There's no doubt about it. You have the imagination of two Jesus Christ's. You wrote science fiction. Now you are going to create a Space Church."

"Yeah, a Space Church. The Space Church of *Joy*."

"How flattering."

"I always say: Credit where credit is due. You are perfectly right. We were all wasting our time writing this hack sci-fi. Now we are putting it into practice!"

"Fully tax-exempted by the IRS. My husband will care for that."

"Horsey!"

There was Horsey standing in the door frame.

Hubbell panicked, "Sorry, Horsey... Joy and I... we were just reading this highly interesting volume by... by..."

He looked at the book cover.

"...by... by... Morris... about the new pope you know... from Russia."

Horsey didn't say a word.

He went to the cabinet, opened it, unscrewed his head and put it on the shelf."

"Are you serious? He's ... a... rowboat... too?"

Joy smiled, "You call him a robot. I call him the perfect husband."

16 Rowboats Dancing in the Moonlight

*"**THAT'S ONE SMALL STEP** for man, one giant leap for mankind,"* Neil's slightly metallic voice was heard on global TV.

Yes, they were on the Moon. It was no fake. The Moon landing on July 20, 1969 was real. No doubt about that. It was not made in a movie studio—although a studio (Distler, who else?) was involved in the overall design of the event.

But Neil Armstrong and Edwin 'Buzz' Aldrin didn't set foot on the Moon, never.

Their robot duplicates manufactured by Distler Engineering did.

Nobody would identify those robots inside a spacesuit.

The history of Distler Robotics began when Walter returned from his trip to Germany. As a gift he was given a little mechanized toy bird. On the outside, it looked like a taxidermy songbird in a cage, but internally it was a machine, which would chirp out music as if it were alive. The first human Distler produced for display at a World's Fair was one of America's leading industrialists, Henry Ford, the founder of the Ford Motor Company. Even after America had entered the war, Ford was still rolling out trucks for the Nazis. Like Hitler Ford hated Jews with a fervent passion. He was convinced that the Jews ruined baseball because they saw money where the sportsman saw fun and skill. According to Ford's anti-Semitic gospel, the Jews were behind everything, from flashy jewelry, white slavery and short skirts to rising rents and the manufacture of cigarettes. There was a Jewish conspiracy going on: a conspiracy to control the world. Hitler insisted that Ford was awarded the Grand Cross of the Supreme Order of the German Eagle.

To beat the Jews, the Nazis claimed, the Führer envisioned an army of robots. The prototypes had already been built.

The robots were among us!

Hitler's fascination with robot life began in his private cinema. In Hitler's vision German people originally were to be transformed into faithful dogs. As is generally known, the Führer was a fanatic dog lover. He had taught Blondi, his German shepherd, a bunch of tricks and delighted in showing of her prowess: "If I can do this to dogs, I can school people too, like dogs."

Then, in August 1934, he was shown a robot movie directed by one of his loyal followers, Harry Piel. Piel had been interested in the topic since he became an *Electric Man* as early as 1915 when he produced, directed and starred as a walking Automaton in the lost *Die grosse Wette (The Big Bet)* that truly can be called Germany's first genuine science fiction movie, long before the term science fiction was invented by Luxembourg-born editor Hugo Gernsback and Czech writer Karel Čapek coined the term *robot* in his play *R.U.R.* Piel joined Hitler's NSDAP in 1933 and became a patron member of the SS. And he went on to produce naïve science fiction at a time when almost all of Hollywood's fantasy films were banned in Germany.

Der Herr der Welt (*Master of the World*) was Harry Piel's second robot film (and the third after Fritz Lang's *Metropolis*): While idealistic factory owner Dr. Heller (Walter Janssen) only wants to create working robots, his colleague, Professor Wolf (Walter Franck), is going to create a gigantic fighting machine as a means to put down strikes and rebellions and secure *world domina-*

tion. Such robots are beneficial—this demonstrates *The Master of the World*—basically for entrepreneurs who are enabled to throw their workers on the dole. Only when an engineer who falls in love at the right time with the right woman, the widow of the robot manufacturer, takes a stand for his workmates, they are regarded: With a share of the profits made from the leasing of the robots they are settled as farmers. While in this half of the story the blessing of technology reached everybody, the fear of technology prevailed in the other half, the horror plot of super robots, a fear that was fed from an experience made in the production process—the experience of the subject being at the mercy of a mechanical object world. Hitler was fascinated by this dichotomy: by the harmless workers' robot as well by its counterpart which he considered the future of warfare.

The screenwriter, Georg Mühlen-Schulte, belonged to a group of authors who had signed an oath of allegiance vowing for Adolf Hitler. The group included Gottfried Benn, Max Halbe, Hanns Johst, Walter von Molo and Will Vesper.

Right before his groundbreaking robot film, Piel turned to another Nazi favorite: TV. In *Die Welt ohne Maske: Ein Film vom Fernsehen (The World Without a Mask: A Film about Television)* two tinkerers, Dr. Tobias Bern (Kurt Vespermann) and his neighbor Harry Palmer (played by Piel himself) accidentally invent fully fledged television: "We not only teleview, we see all through!" The invention enables the two to see right through walls. That was something. "Just imagine," Hitler said when he watched the movie, it gave him the idea of "seeing not only through walls but through people too and know what they carry in the heads."

Mind control by TV, robotic assembly-line work and weaponized robots. "This is clearly the future, the second revolution in warfare, gentlemen, after gunpowder."

"But robots do not have emotions influencing decisions," one of his generals objected.

"The only one who is going to make decisions will be *ME*. Therefore, it is imperative to save my brain for posterity once I'm dead."

"But how, my Führer? How can this be done?"

"By brain surgery, General Keitel. Tonight, we are going to watch an American movie: *Frankenstein*! Only a German genius like that of Dr. Frankenstein could accomplish this task. The history of medicine is going to immortalize me so that all can obey my orders even after my physical body's death. And I tell you: We have the German genius to follow in the steps of Paracelsus and Dr. Frankenstein."

"Who? Who is it, my Führer?"

"Professor Dr. Julius Hallervorden. Dr. Hallervorden and his assistants, Dr. Gustav Ziska and Tristan Todt. We only have to provide the guinea pigs... from our concentration camps. You see, gentlemen, concentration camps make sense for we need fresh blood and—brains."

This conviction was in accordance with the Hallervorden doctrine. "If you are going to kill prisoners, mein Führer," he advised Hitler, "at least take the brains out so that the material can be utilized."

"How many can you examine, Herr Professor?"

"An unlimited number—the more the better, mein Führer! The creation of an Aryan race requires eliminating everything and everyone who does not fit this mold. We must be as hard and brutal as Nature itself."

Hitler agreed, "*Einverstanden*, Herr Professor."

Hallervorden provided the fixatives, jars and boxes, and instructions for removing and fixing the brains. It didn't take long before they came bringing brains in like a delivery van from the furniture company. Hallervorden was mad with joy. In retrospect: "There was wonderful material among those brains, beautiful mental-defectives, mal-formations and early infantile diseases. The SS was highly efficient and professional. I gladly accepted these brains, of course I did. Where they came from and how they came to me was really none of my business." In the years to come Hallervorden and his assistants received hundreds, thousands of brains, many of them Jewish. The Jews had to die so that the Führer would live—forever. It was out of respect for human life, these scientists argued, that they would remove a gangrenous appendix from a diseased body. And Jews were considered the gangrenous appendix in the body of mankind. It was that "easy".

Society was viewed as a human body that needed to be "pure". Nazi medicine therefore aimed to erase "impurities" from the human race. Particularly Hallervorden's assistant Todt went so far as if choosing people to be murdered in order to advance his research. Todt was sent to specific killing facilities to teach physicians what diagnoses they were seeking and how to remove the brains efficiently.

As a robot, Horsey had the most important prerequisite an actor could have. He had a photographic memory. He always knew his text and therefore was able to pretend to speak freely and monitor his audiences closely for their reactions to everything that came out of his mouth. He didn't know what he was saying but he knew when a line had landed powerfully. He realized when his speech had persuaded them. He could register it in their eyes.

TV would do the rest and lay the foundation of American-way mind control.

On April 20, 1950, a Project under the name of *Bluebird* had been approved by the director of the CIA. Practical research was to be conducted to include these specific questions:

- Can we create by post-hypnotic control an action contrary to an individual's basic moral principle?
- Can we create in a matter of an hour or two a hypnotic condition in an unwilling subject to such extent that he will perform an act for our benefit?

- Could we seize a subject and in the space of an hour or two by post-hypnotic control have him crash an airplane, wreck a train, etc.?
- Can we, applying techniques of hypnosis and sleep inducing, force a subject to travel long distances, commit specified acts such as sabotage and return to us certain documents or materials?
- Can we devise a system for making unwilling subjects into willing agents and then transfer that control to untrained agency agents in the field by use of codes or identifying signs?
- Can we "alter" a person's personality?

Physicians secretly gave soldier volunteers synthetic marijuana, LSD and two dozen other psychoactive drugs but found that acid and pot were either too unpredictable or too mellow to be useful. They experimented with hallucinogenic weapons such as softball-size artillery rounds that were filled with powdered quinuclidinyl benzilate or BZ, a deliriant of the belladonnoid family that had placed some research subjects in a sleeplike state and left them impaired for days.

But Hitler's scientists knew that TV would do a much better job and that experiments could be easier conducted under the roof of a huge corporation than with a democratic state involved.

The world we see is highly illusionary. It is filled with intent to sell us on products, services, public figures and political agendas. Our vision is saturated with stimulating images, repeated over and over again, while our minds are chemically suppressed with addictive drugs, from over-the-counter medicines to soda pop. The final objective of these mind control mechanisms is an automated, mindless society.

Robot he was, Governor Horsey was thrilled to bits when Von, within weeks of sending Neil Armstrong and his fellow robots successfully to the Moon in July 1969 and creating national euphoria, devised the plan for a Mars mission to start in November 1981. The plan involved four key elements. These comprised the Saturn V, Nuclear Shuttle, Mars Mission Module and a Mars Excursion Module for a single flight to Mars and back.

The mission would begin in Earth orbit by clustering three Nuclear Shuttles in parallel. The central core Nuclear Shuttle would carry a Mission Module on top, to the front of which was attached the Mars Exploration Module within a protective shroud. The two outer Nuclear Shuttle boost stages would detach after accelerating to escape velocity, returning to Earth orbit where they could be used again. Von calculated that it would take nine months to get to the Red Planet. During the flight the crew of three would have lived in a spacious habitat, a cylindrical section 7.7m in diameter and 12.7m in length, a pressurized volume incorporating four decks, with access to each via a central tunnel that could serve as refuge in the event of a solar storm. After ten weeks in Mars orbit the crew members were supposed to make the trip to the surface in the Excursion Module.

Both stood outside on the veranda of Horsey's house and watched the nightly sky. Horsey would have liked to volunteer, being one of three robots, but Von stopped him with a wave of his hand.

"You will be more valuable to our Program of Purification on Earth, not on Mars! You are our best promoter and we don't like to lose you in a meteor shower or solar storm. We need your speech on the stage of politics."

"But you got Tricky Dick."

"Yeah." Von screwed up his nose. "But this man is beyond control. We tried to inspire him but found that this man is a prey to drink, drugs and fits of rage. He washes a variety of pills down with a glass of scotch or a couple martinis. Last month his close buddy, "Bebe", and a few others arrived at the White House at 2 a.m. with a mysterious trunk that they insisted was for the President. When the Secret Service opened it, there was a naked stripper inside, holding a bottle of champagne. When the President is drunk, he kills the time by listening to his own recordings of White House conversations. While all of this is forgivable, we cannot accept his ties with Carlos Marcello and the Mafia. No, we need a Republican we can bank on."

"But after I did as I am told you must promise that you send me to Mars. I must meet my Martian brothers."

Although he had been transformed into a robot, there was still enough emotion that moved Horsey. He was still connected in a strange way to his original head and brain that were safely stored somewhere in the depths of Disterland's vast warehouses.

Von smiled, "Promise—*after* mission is accomplished."

"It's a deal, Von. I am very glad."

17 Hitler Competition on German Screens

THE OLD BAVARIAN farmer was speechless. His stogie dropped out of his mouth.

Instinctively he extended his arm and saluted *Heil Hitler*.

Hitler smiled and greeted him back, *"Bon giorno!"*

Born giorno? Why should Hitler speak Italian? And why was he still alive?

The same time Von helped to bring Americans to the Moon and back, a little producer in what had remained after the lost war of the original *Land of Hate* (that's what the late author Heinrich Mann had called his native country) released a sex film comedy with Adolf Hitler. He had hired a little Italian to play the part of the Führer. However, Renato Rinaldini had to be dubbed for the role as his German wasn't sufficient.

Born in 1926, small in stature, perspiring, dumpy, a shrewd wheeler-dealer, a perfect reincarnation of Hitler's favorite Munich comedian Weiss Ferdl, producer Ade (Bavarian for Adolf!) Brunner had served as Josef Mengele's personal driver at Auschwitz Concentration Camp. Like most Germans after the war, he felt not guilty, *"Ich befolgte nur meine Befehle.—I only obeyed orders."* He became a hauler but never dreamed to enter the movie business of the doomed inmates and their guards. Although—his spare time in Auschwitz he had used to make home movies, footage that he would later sell to various TV stations. Anyway, he inherited two cinemas from a debitor. Soon he opened his own distribution company, AB Films, releasing cheap softcore sex comedies and finally decided to become a producer.

And as he was the son of a farmer, he didn't use expensive regular film sets but those familiar farms and cow barns he found in the Bavarian villages around Munich. Even hay carts were used for nude love scenes. Of course, he didn't tell the farmers that he produced sex films. He just told them that he shot funny pictures: *Heimatfilme* so to speak, popular sentimental films in idealized regional settings.

If a farmer got wary and realized during shooting that amidst his cows some girls took off their clothes, his conscience was silenced by paying him some more money. Afterwards the papist wife of the farmer, for any eventuality, would care that the sullied location was radically purged by the village priest with pious blessing and holy water. The priest didn't ask questions although rumors spread like wildfire. Some small donation, a basket filled with eggs and a charitable break adjusted everything.

On location the producer always arrived in his White Mercedes. He had a bundle of banknotes in his trousers pocket and no problems to contract with the respective farmers.

The girls got appointments to show up right on location. However, not the cow barns were what they were shown first but the film crew with the whole enchilada, the 35 mm camera, the lighting equipment, and other ladies who acted *dressed* in front of this camera. When the aspirants had gazed enough in amazement without becoming suspicious, they were asked if they would take part or not. Most of them were more than willing. Some of them felt a secret urge in their breast to become a screen goddess. They had to sign a pre-formulated contract. Most didn't even bother to read what they signed on the hood of or inside the producer's Mercedes. The usual standard terms were changed to the detriment of the girls. Including all rights, they were given a shabby payment of 50 Marks daily. The producer was in the clear.

After a while, it came to cinematic light that the girls were expected to *undress* for their appearance in these funny, harmless *Heimatfilms*. To calm them down they were offered a slightly higher rate for the extra service. Girls who cast off their clothes got a daily rate of *100* Marks, not much either. The contracts, hastily signed, disappeared immediately in the briefcase of the location manager who signaled the producer with a vulpine look that the girl was caught in the trap. With a sanctimonious smile, the female applicants were congratulated on their decision.

Often the girls brought along their girlfriends. When these realized where they had run aground, some friendship broke up.

All options of a successful casting were exploited. Besides ads, some applicants were placed by dubious small agencies. The girls were regarded as nothing else than meat stock. They didn't have the slightest chance of a real, honest career, but they were good enough as cannon fodder for the wave of exploitation and sex films. For some of the aspiring actresses their participation in such crap later became a calamity job wise. Instead of reaching their dream destination, nothing else remained than a sour aftertaste and bitterness. They were typecast, without any chance of getting parts in serious films.

Nevertheless, there were even mothers who sacrificed their innocent, naïve daughters and brought them to the casting. These girls were expected to fulfill their mothers' lifelong dream and start a solid career as starlet.

Another trick was purposeful recruitment. The producer sent his sleuths onto Munich streets. They were lying in wait in front of schools, universities, bars, discos, public swimming pools, attended parties and so on. Where there was a chance to capture a lot of booty for the camera, they were lurking. Housewives were in demand, too, who wanted to bump up the meager salary of their husbands or who felt bored and unsatisfied at home and were looking for an "adventure".

This way a file was compiled. It was worth a mint: contacts, addresses and phone numbers, horses for courses. Location and production managers kept the record and for some extra charge imparted their knowledge to other production companies.

On location, the girls were treated well and diplomatically. Ade tried to convey to the girls in his robust, slightly nasal Bavarian dialect what it was all about. When he had no more arguments and began to feel uncomfortable in his skin, he abandoned the conversation abruptly: "Will you take part now? Yes, or no?"

As soon as his shrewd instinct sensed a certain disposition, he threw the female applicants in at the deep end and explained what came up to them: "We are making a funny sex film. We need a few girls who are willing to take off bra and panties and stand a little nude in front of the camera." He finished the sentence: "Well then, will you take part? You will have fun. We are like a family."

There was no problem to convince the girls to take off their bras. The slip was a bigger problem. There were complaints and trouble. Take for instance a bedroom scene: Who is going to bed to make love in panties? For the cameramen the panties offered technical problems of their own. How to avoid showing panties with a little streak? So they talked to the girls until they were softened up and willing. An additional blue banknote worked sometimes miracles.

Each minute cost money. Film stock was saved. Three rehearsals, at most two takes. So: hush! hush! The woman lay naked, you were atop, some petting, kissing... then expertly swinging between her legs without revealing genitalia and pubic hair.

The mating began either gently or in hectic rabbit speed.

Important was to get them undressed voluntarily. The main problem concerning the girls were the million eyes of spectators watching with voyeuristic grin. The production tried its best to reduce the staff to a minimum: cameraman and assistant, director and assistant, one gaffer, a make-up man—no more than six persons who acted as professionally as possible.

If they found out that a girl was underage, she was substituted immediately to avoid trouble with government agencies and families. Many parents didn't know in what type of dirty *Schmuddelecke* their daughters had repaired to. These young girls didn't have much life experience.

The fees were paid off daily after shooting. This was psychologically effective because the banknotes were remedy for the wounds of the sensitive creatures. Shooting schedules lasted on average 25 days. Main parts were paid roughly 2,500 Marks.

But back to Brunner's favorite actor Renato Rinaldini, the Italian Adolf Hitler. Rinaldini had come as a migrant worker, a *Gastarbeiter* from San Benedetto del Tronto to Munich in the mid-1960s:

One novice film director had seen me and brought me to Munich Pasing to meet the producer. When he opened the door, a perfumed whiff almost knocked me down.

In front of me, I saw a burly man in a white shirt, silk grey trousers, black slippers and with thin hair combed backwards. In his moon face I realized the flash of a gold tooth. He shook my hand. In the other hand he had a framed black and white photo which showed a rundown clochard. The caption read: "He gave the highest discount." I didn't understand but the director whom we called Hähnchen [Chicken] whispered and explained I shouldn't be "too expensive" and shouldn't make "demands". The man, who feared to transform into a clochard if he didn't save the money for himself, was Ade Brunner. My contract was ready to sign. I needed the money. Our first child was born. So naïvely I signed.

The market was starving for that type of moronism.

Rinaldini: *I felt like being on the beach of a tropical island. The spotlights heated the set by 40 degrees. Fast I had overcome my inhibitions. Not only did I hop without a stitch on in front of the camera but made a contribution to help the girls overcome their inhibitions to strip, too. As born Arlecchino (Harlequin) I got the nickname "Mister Klamottini" (Klamotte = cheap farce).*

With Ade Brunner, teams and all male actors had to restrain themselves. He was angst-ridden that his house might be dismissively called a brothel. It was supposed to substitute for no more than a cheap studio. Booze was strictly forbidden, smoking too. One who wouldn't observe the rules was fired immediately. The catering consisted of sausage, headcheese, hard rolls, and pretzel, to drink only lemonade and water.

Good and professional actors and actresses weren't available for that kind of job. What remained was C grade at most. Well-known postwar actors took care to prevent from being confused with this type of production and kept distance—in spite of the frustratingly low fees at the theater. I didn't bother about acting, at least not at that time, and didn't care that I was typecast in a genre that ranked lowest in high culture.

Later when this wave of films had become mainstream, some more illustrious actresses and actors overcame their reservations and dared to participate. They jumped, so to speak, from the pan into the fire, will say: out of personal financial calamities into an awkward situation damaging what was left of their reputation.

Undress, dress—again and again... There was no room for professional acting. Those who succeeded in turning a producer's or director's head did a small career leap but it was rather ephemeral.

The agitation in the bed at group sex was more than distressing. No trace of sex. But who cared? The audience wasn't that sophisticated. They just wanted to laugh, see some flesh and attractive girls.

Whether blond or brown, the girls looked terrific. The original hair color didn't matter when they were hired. But when there was a shortage of girls, they opened their bag of tricks and used wigs to disguise an actress and have one and the same girl in a dual role. That meant also: twice as much fee.

Most "actresses" who were pushed into such dual or even triple roles were office assistants or housewives. Enough makeup and wigs were available. Itinerary laborers preferred to see German blondies, if possible, Valkyries. The main point was that the naked women could move naturally and pretend a natural moaning.

Not only the "actresses" were double, sometimes even the movies led a double life. Thanks to smart contracts that defined all rights in his interest, Brunner was able to recycle and change the complete footage as the whim took them. He tattered two movies in a way that he got a third one without spending a dime.

When the "actresses" saw themselves for the first time on the screen, some of them giggled while others were ashamed.

Back in the 1970s, it was all the rave to smoke joints while the kids of the upper class inhaled their lines of coke. In the film industry it was not different. Many saw a chance to gain control that way of inhibitions and other problems. When almost everybody smoked—hippies, musicians, creative artists, even politicians— and cabaret artist Wolfgang Neuss proclaimed that on German soil never more a joint should burn out, hash and pot were shopped around the cheap soft sex lots. But after a while, I quit because I had no desire for such things.

Around us blazed something like a cultural revolution: music, art, hippie and APO protesters, sexual revolution—that was drowned in petit bourgeois consumption.

The drugs were supplied by two of Brunner's cheap assistants. Mario Montini was no Italian but he thought that an Italian name was sweet with the air of Renaissance. Of course, he was not born in Renaissance. He was raised on a farm in the Berchtesgaden area and had heard a lot about the Führer from his mother who had delivered breakfast eggs to Hitler's Berghof residence: a biography to Brunner's liking. But Mom didn't imagine her boy working on the sets of sex films. She would have liked to see him become a priest on the stages of the Catholic Church. To please her Mario adopted the stage name Montini, after Pope Paul VI., who was born Montini. His real name was something like Siegwin Schüller.

Mario had no formal training at all. In Bottrop he had worked as kung fu instructor in a shabby gym. That was all but he was alert and very ambitious and, besides, a gifted photographer. Hähnchen had introduced him to the producer and got him the job. To Brunner he became stills photographer, janitor, butler, and location manager, all in one person. Brunner who had definitely no taste even let Mario select black suite for the interior sets in his villa in Pasing. Eventually Mario Montini became Brunner's right-hand man. He was pale, of medium size, dark blond, sideward parted, well-tended, with blue eyes behind yellowish Ray Ban glasses, state-of-the-art in those days. He wore tight light-colored jeans, a white or green Lacoste T-shirt, white moccasins or white sneakers. Above all, thanks to Martial Arts training, he had well-developed muscles and fast reflexes.

The moment a girl came near to him Mario began to beam. The name of his girlfriend was Mariandl. Mariandl Kunstdorf was pretty as a picture and sympathetic but they quarreled all time because Mario was such a womanizer. Enthusiastically, he photographed anything that happened on the set with his Rolex camera. Of course, he caused non-stop trouble. But most often, Mario managed to pull a Pinocchio and squirm free. Thus, things were settled.

When the producer included him in his team, he extended his responsibility. Mario was allowed to work on the screenplay and sit down next to the camera and read aloud the lines. That system worked perfectly as they didn't use original soundtrack but shot silent and the rest was left to post-dubbing.

When Mario was promoted assistant director, a new stills photographer popped up. This second assistant, Balder Deich, was not very popular with the girls or Montini but he had attended one or two courses at the newly founded Film & TV School in

Munich. From then on, he claimed to know all about movie making. Balder, we heard of him before when he was "Uncle" Albin's boy somewhere in Hoyerswerda, East Germany. Now Balder was tall, slim, dark-haired and very Bavarian.

Together Ade's assistants matched the ideal Hitler had in mind for the German youth: Mario claimed for himself to be as tough as leather and as hard as Krupp's steel. Balder, on the other hand, was as swift as a greyhound and used his camera in a pushy way because he was determined to get alluring erotic subjects for the posters.

Brunner had the full attention of his assistants, when he talked about Hitler. As a child, then years before he became Josef Mengele's chauffeur, Ade had seen Adolf Hitler in person. He was in a group of summer vacationists when Hitler's car would stop. The Führer got out and asked for the boy's name. Ade would tell him that his name was the same as Hitler's. Hitler seemed pleased and patted on Ade's head, "*Nur weiter so, Adolf! Wir Namensvettern müssen zusammenhalten!!*—Just carry on, Adolf! Us name twins must stick together!!" Decades after that memorable encounter, Ade could still smell Hitler's sudden fart and trump and wondered what the other Adolf had for lunch. He was sure that the Führer had let one go when he returned to his car—as if to confirm the pact between him and the boy.

To Brunner, it was a specific legacy to erect a cinematic memorial in Adolf's honor. He had written the screenplay himself and described the first time Adolf had sex with Eva. Rinaldini's Hitler would hump an Eva Braun lookalike in a hay barn beneath Hitler's original Obersalzberg with all kind of animals, cows, dogs and sheep, shitting around. Eva was played by Mario's girlfriend Mariandl.

Mariandl had the most magnificent line a German actress could have. At least that was what Ade thought.

"Mein Führer," she was heard saying. "You only got one ball!!!"

There had been long speculation that Hitler was missing one testicle. Rumors circulated that he had lost the other one during the Battle of the Somme. But Ade knew better. He knew the true reason of Hitler's monarchism. As a kid the future Führer peed into a billy goat's mouth. The goat took immediate revenge and bit off one of his balls.

Originally, Brunner had even added a scene with a goat that scares Rinaldini away from his love camp. The comedy scene was shot in high speed but cut out just before release because some of Ade's war comrades called it blasphemy after the preview.

"You can't do that, Ade. You can't pull our Führer's leg. You can't make HIM a slapstick Hanswurst."

"But they will love our Führer in such a funny scene."

"They shall not love him. They shall *fear* him."

That was the end of Hitler's slapstick scene. But even without it there was not much to fear about that Hitler impersonation anyway.

Of course, Brunner had to change the title from *The Secret Love Life of Our Beloved Führer* to *Hitler and his Salzberg Girl*. (The "Ober" was left out of Salzberg.) The critics, if they stooped so low to see and review it at all, had nothing nice to say about Hitler and his loyal Brunner, but the German audience stormed the box office and made the cheap hay-barn production the smash hit of the year.

The box-office receipts were that promising that others would jump on the bandwagon, except for the nude scenes.

Hitler celebrated a comeback.

In 1973, a voluminous book was published that became an instant bestseller: Joachim C. Fest's work brought German Fascism exclusively down to one man—*Hitler*.

In 1977, the Berlin Film Festival screened the corresponding documentary: *Hitler: A Career* by Fest and Christian Herrendoerfer that made Hitler a star again on German screens, as he once had been in *Triumph of the Will*. Consequently, many clips were taken from Helen Bertha's infamous Party Rally film. German audiences lined up around the block to see the movie. They wouldn't listen to the scattered voices of critics like filmmaker Wim Wenders who saw it at the Berlin International Film Festival and was aghast:

The bill in hands, filled with strong declarations, I had high expectations seeing the film. I read: "This film presents Hitler's time unprejudicedly, objectively and rationally. It conveys the fascination of Hitler's career without giving in to the temptation to sink beneath the weight of it.

"This film doesn't manipulate our history. It doesn't glorify and idealize. It explains." Why to defend something that hadn't been attacked yet?

My astonishment was justified as soon as the film began, and it grew into disbelieving bewilderment. When it was over, there was some brief applause, then the usually forceful festival audience skedaddled, puzzled, and embarrassed. One made a joke, "That's Entertainment, Part 3", but it was no release.

Wenders felt obliged to talk about this *Unfilm,* mis-film, as one who made movies in Germany: *I speak up for all who in the past years, after a long blankness, began again to produce images and sounds in a country that is prepossessed with an abysmal distrust of images and sounds that tell of it, that on this account for 30 years anxiously absorbed all foreign images if only they distracted from itself. I don't believe that anywhere there is such a loss of trust in the own images, the own stories and myths as with us. We, the directors of New German Cinema, have sensed this loss plainest considering the lack, the absence of own tradition, growing up fatherless, and we sensed it in the helplessness and the initial reserve of the viewers. Only slowly, this defensive attitude on one side and the lack of self-confidence crumbled away, and in a process that maybe might last years, a feeling is developing here again that images and sounds don't need to be imported but should talk about this country and could come from this country.*

There is good reason for this distrust for nowhere else images and voice were used that unscrupulously as in this country, never before and nowhere else they were so vulgarized for the transport of lies. And now there comes a film that, with unfathomable rashness, wants to sell these images as the crux of the matter and as "documentary footage", DOES SELL, and therefore, ONCE AGAIN, transports some lies.

The "career" Fest und Herrendoerfer are going to comprehend was made possible not least because there was a total control about any foot of film footage, because all images that exist of this man and his ideas were ingeniously made, skillfully selected and utilized purposefully. Because of this demagogically dealing with images, all who responsibly and competently had to do with images in Germany left this country. For their "comprehensive documentary" Fest and Herrendoerfer therefore only can refer, with few exceptions, to the images of fellow travelers, to the view of accomplices, propaganda stuff that is, the most swinish feet of film ever exposed. All of this they absorb uncritically, don't draw the slightest consequences for their method of operating. They have the effrontery to write the introduction: "For this film no scene was reconstructed", smarten it even up at most, inflate and double the propaganda value occasionally and make themselves subsequently to instruments.

Once again: Because of these images which we are watching for two hours there was a hole of thirty to forty years in the cinematic culture of this country. Fest and Herrendoerfer tear it open again with a smile taking pride in their horrible discoveries. Against what is oozing out they are counterposing nothing else than a commentary.

This film is fascinated by its own object, by the importance of that object in which it participates ("He proves the truth of the word that history sometimes likes to take shape in a SINGLE man."), so that this object takes over, becomes its own narrator.

In 1940 a sentimental Hitler had told Helen Bertha who had created a lot of the footage later sold for a good price to Fest and

Herrendoerfer: "*It would be marvelous if one could watch films from the past today, films about Frederic the Great, Napoleon and the historical events of ancient Greece.*" Fate fortunately (?) provided enough film footage that showed *him* in the best light.

Hitler was absolutely convinced that he had a camera face. He always said, "There are so many good-looking, handsome people around me but the eye of the camera dislikes them all. It's totally different when I enter the scene and get a close up. From that moment on it's a love affair between the camera and me. The most famous face in history will be mine."

Fest and Herrendoerfer had become fascinated by that most famous face in history—but not only them. Some young German filmmakers were downright obsessed with Hitler as well. Hans Jürgen Syberberg, an eccentric outsider among Germany's young filmmakers, produced *Winifred Wagner und die Geschichte des Hauses Wahnfried*. Frau Wagner, direct quote, "*If Hitler would come through that door today, I would be as happy to see him here and have him here as ever...*" After that, Syberberg felt qualified enough to offer, the same year Fest's film was released, an almost Wagnerian *Film aus Deutschland* (*A film from Germany*): *Hitler* (world-wide title: <u>Our</u> *Hitler*) in four parts between 90 and 120 minutes each, produced for a low-budget of (estimated) one million mark by nobody else than Balder Deich who went on his own after Brunner's sudden death. It was not clear if Brunner had been killed and pushed from the roof of his villa or if he went atop to complain about some roofer's repair job and deduct some dimes from the invoice.

Where Deich and Syberberg got the budget from is not exactly clear. State film funding in those days was scarce. TV represented by Westdeutscher Rundfunk Cologne and BBC London put in some money but it wasn't enough. Deich, however, knew some old Hitler fans who were eager to put up the money.

The critical reaction to the Deich-produced film from Germany had been mixed. Syberberg met with almost universal rejection in Germany and with much, at times enthusiastic, acclaim outside Germany particularly in America and in France, where his film was hailed as *Faust, Part III*. Susan Sontag wrote a passionately partisan yet greatly illuminating essay about the film in *The New York Review of Books*. She judged it a masterpiece of "unprecedented ambition."

Mario Montini was eaten up with envy when he learned that his rival Balder was producing a Hitler movie ahead of him. He immediately took action and phoned the new rising star among Young German filmmakers, Rainer Werner Fassbinder. Like Andy Warhol, Fassbinder had his own "factory" and always needed money to finance his and his friends' consumption of Bavarian beer, radish and cocaine. Drunk as a skunk, he agreed to create a picture tentatively titled *Mario Montini Proudly Presents Rainer Werner Fassbinder's Hitler*. Of course, Fassbinder had no time to write the screenplay himself. Kurt Raab, who liked to be compared to Peter Lorre of *M* fame because he recently had played serial killer Fritz Haarmann, the "Vampire of Hanover", in Fassbinder's *Tenderness of the Wolves* in 1973, was given the doubtful chance to write the script and play Hitler for peanuts. Rinaldini who applied for the job too was sent away as he wasn't considered a consummate pro.

There was an interesting observation once made by Klaus Mann, the son of Thomas: In 1932, Klaus sat, by pure chance, next to Herr Hitler in the tea room of the Munich Carlton Hotel. All of a sudden, he believed to recognize in Hitler's "pathological" physiognomy the features of Fritz Haarmann, the mass murderer who was executed in April 1925. Under such premises, *Fassbinder's Hitler* could have been an unusual picture, but on the first day of shooting Fassbinder was so drunk that his vassal Ulli Lommel had to take over. Ulli fabricated nothing else than a cheap farce, not the slightest the way Chaplin, Lubitsch or Monty Python (*Mr. Hilter*) did. We hear Raab (*sans* Hitler beard) barking, see him crawling on all fours or playing Battleship, listening to Wagner's

Rienzi that allegedly inspired the original to become Germany's next dictator. We also see a group of soldierly male bodies and a choir of Hitler Youth singing *Guten Abend, gut' Nacht.* In between, Raab's Hitler longs for Marlene Dietrich and asks Goebbels (played by a totally miscast Lommel) to lure her back to Germany. This idea was based on facts, however: Ufa indeed tried to interest freshly baked Hollywood Marlene to do a few films in Germany again, for 100,000 Reichsmark per movie, but Marlene turned the Germans down. Margit Carstensen played Marlene. Critic Wolfgang Limmer wrote that she tried honestly to live up to Marlene's singing voice, but in the end radiated the sex appeal of a coat-tree.

Fassbinder distanced himself from the movie, called it fascistic, but there was no way to cut out his minor but totally convincing acting part as morphine-addicted Hermann Göring.

In spite of what Wim Wenders had written, these young German filmmakers were so dazzled by the Third Reich that they vomited cinematic barf of the kind Mel Brooks had parodied in his movie *The Producers*: In Germany it was really *Springtime for Hitler*! One night, Fassbinder and Montini walked arm in arm singing the Horst Wessel song. *He was no Fascist,* Mario excused. *He was just interested, as a homosexual, in the male society of the SA.*

Both movies, neither the one produced by Balder nor Mario's, were up to Hitler's legacy. Finally, Montini and Deich had a meeting of minds and agreed to produce a bigger, the *definitive* Hitler epic that would stand the test of time. It was supposed to not have to shun any comparison with William Shakespeare's immortal plays, with *Macbeth* or *The Tragedy of King Richard the Third*.

Bloody thou art, bloody will be thy end...

Montini suggested to get American director John Milius on board. Milius was a die-hard militarist. He had co-written *Apocalypse Now* with Francis Ford Coppola and added the *Ride of the*

Valkyries from Richard Wagner's 1870 *Die Walküre* to the Helicopter attack opening. War was to become an opera: *"I love the smell of napalm in the morning."*

An overly enthusiastic Milius sent Montini a fax and pathetically exclaimed that he was in the starting holes already wearing his German steel helmet. They had rejected Milius as unfit for service. Milius shed crocodile tears, "It was totally demoralizing. I'd had given anything to be a Marine. As a surfer I've spent a lot of time hanging out with the Marines off Pendleton, and I'd had every intention of joining up. But I was a case of sometimes disabling mild asthma and they rejected me. Didn't send me to Vietnam. Shit! I missed going to my war. This probably caused me to be obsessed with war ever since. At least on the screen. To make a movie about your Führer and WW2 would be a dream coming true."

But before that dream came true, the German producers were asked to meet John's fee of half a million. Milius was not only a militarist. He also was a shrewd businessman. That was way too much.

Fortunately, Deich had another ace up in his sleeve. Why not ask an original Nazi director who definitely would do it for half-price? His friend from film school days, "Herman the German", an intellectual four-eyes from the Lower Rhine Valley where his family ran a clothing store, had interviewed old Helen Bertha and since then was close to her ass. Helen Bertha was not only a personal friend of the late Führer, she had produced his most famous film as we know: *Triumph of the Will*. A new Hitler film directed by that woman would be reviewed as absolutely "authentic". No question about that. The Third Reich could be only picturized by a loyal German not by a makeshift American militarist (and Jew) like John Milius.

Thus, negotiations began with Helen Bertha. Immediately, Balder Deich mobilized Munich's yellow press asking for headlines that "we got *HER*"—which sounded like next to *HIM*.

As David Selznick way back in the late 1930s tested many actresses for the part of Scarlett O'Hara (excluding Helen Bertha), Montini and Deich (or, Deich and Montini) spared no efforts and pain to test a phalanx of German actors for the Hitler part. Only Rinaldini was sent away then and there.

Helen Bertha objected to them all. She insisted that there was only one person around able to play Hitler—and that was Hitler himself!

"But he is dead," the producers tried to intervene.

"No, he isn't. He still appears in my dreams. At least twice a week."

"Yes, Helen. In your dreams and in the dreams of many a German but…"

"No, no, he assured me that he is doing well and living in Hollywood?"

"Hollywood?"

Helen Bertha spoke the magic word. Why only Germany if it could be Hollywood!

"My uncle… Uncle Albin, you know…"

They didn't know. Balder had to explain, "Uncle Albin… he is a retired Bundeswehr general."

"Na und?"

"And he worked as a military consultant on many Hollywood movies. Maybe… He is close to the Distler Organization."

"Distler?" Mario asked him to contact this Uncle immediately.

"If anyone knows where to find the Führer and Hollywood money, it's my Uncle Albin."

Albin put in a few phone calls and then they got an appointment with some vice president of Distler's releasing company, Buena Noche.

Thanks to Albin's advocacy and after reviewing the screenplay, Buena Noche was indeed *very* interested in that new *Hitler* picture they were offered as they had missed out on *Stars at War*, the new hit movie made by a guy named Georg Lukas, something or else. What could be better than *Stars at War* than *WW2 the Original*.

They agreed to release it—provided they would sign the greatest name in Distler's Organization.

"Who is that?"

"The Governor of California."

"You mean: Horsey?"

18 Hit the Lukas, or WWII in Outer Space

MEANWHILE, a fresh new wind blew in Hollywood.

World War in Outer Space!

What else was *Stars at War* in its original packing than WW2 in Outer Space? Many of the X-winged VFX elements seen on the silver screen in 1977 were modeled frame by frame copying footage from dogfights taken from Nazi newsreels and from *The Dam Busters*, a 1955 British war film that described an air raid of Avro Lancaster Bombers against a dam which contained the Lake Möhne (May 16/17, 1943). *...one of the key visions I had of the film when I started,* Lukas said, *was of a dogfight in outer space with spaceships—two ships flying through space shooting at each other. That was my original idea.*

To a World War II history buff, the iconic Millennium Falcon from *Stars at War* resembles one of the best-known bombers of all time.

The greenhouse cockpit configuration, along with the gun turrets, aboard the ship was lifted straight out of the blueprints for the Boeing B-29 Superfortress.

The Superfortress was a workhorse of the U.S. Army Air Forces that was best known for dropping atomic bombs on the Japanese cities of Hiroshima and Nagasaki.

Stars at War creator Georg Lukas was known to have studied 20 to 25 hours of footage from World War II dogfights while doing research for the film. Footage of World War II dogfights was even used as a placeholder before the special effects were edited into the original film.

The shooting for the very first *Stars at Wars*, today *Episode IV* according to the gospel of the saga, took place in 1975, the year of the fall of Saigon that marked the end of the Vietnam War. On August 9, 1974, Richard M. Nixon had resigned and became immortal as the role model for the *Stars at War* Imperator who split family ties.

Robert Blalack and his special effects printer, a leftover machine from a Columbia picture titled *Marooned*, had been an important part of the original project:

20th Century-Fox had no idea how much the Stars at War never-been-done Visual Effects would cost. But Fox knew it had a contract with the Hollywood Unions that required every hour worked on Fox movies to be Union. After 40 hours, Time and ½. After 50 hours, Double Time or "Golden Time". After 60 hours, Triple Time. Each hour frosted with a 37% Pension, Welfare and Vacation surcharge.

Fox's minimalist budget demanded the invention of a shell corporation, called Industrial Light & Magic, funded by Fox to function as the arms-length Non-Union Employer of the Stars at War VFX workers. These non-Union VFX workers were to all be paid a fixed weekly "salary", a fraction of the 40-hour base-pay of their Union counterparts. The Stars at War VFX work menu was for many a 6 day, 60 to 80-hour week, no Overtime, zero Union Pension and Welfare and Vacation pay.

With the VFX projected to cost 300% less than if the horrid Union VFX workers did the movie, it was a studio gamble worth a roll of the dice, even if it went over budget, which it did.

With experienced Union VFX workers out of the equation, the VFX labor pool was drawn from young artists and Nixon's Vietnam

Vets who were infatuated with movies and had nothing to lose. None of the VFX crew had ever worked on a Visual Effects movie of this scale. Most had never worked on any Hollywood movie.

When Stars at War *began shooting its Live Action out of England, we started creating from scratch the photographic tools and processes of a revolutionary VFX studio, in an empty warehouse in Van Nuys, California.*

After 14 months, with 10 months to the finish line, the photographic VFX system we created had its wrinkles ironed out. 1 of 365 shots was finished. $1 million of the $1.6 million VFX budget was gone. Lukas and his VFX Supervisor Dykstra mix like a librarian and a Hells Angel. A Hatchet Man arrived on cue to fire Dykstra and discipline the too-arty non-Union crew. We tell Hatchet if Dykstra goes, we go, so Dykstra stays, while Hatchet Man plays combo marriage counselor and Consigliere.

The hysteria of the Fox people about the movie's Over Budget, mixed with its terror that Distler made the Smart Choice to turn the Lukas project down, eventually convinced them to give Lukas the Toy and Sequel rights in exchange for not killing the movie, but only if the filmmakers paid $2 for every $1 the movie was over budget from their share of any box-office profits.

Georg Lukas, inspired by none other than Distler, Von and Hitler himself or better: Hitler's cheap clone Nixon, as well as old *Flash Gordon* serials, Stanley Kubrick's *2001* and Von's NASA visions that had relapsed after the Moon landing in 1969, made millions just from the merchandise.

The Distler Organization didn't mind. "We are going to buy that Lukas guy later." More important to them was the understanding that time was ripe to turn *Stars at War* into reality. And Horsey who had seen the movie and liked it was to be the prophet to accomplish the task. Not many people knew that Georg Lukas had approached him to play Obi-Wan Kenobi, but Distler didn't want to see him connected with a rival project and besides that, having been Governor of California, he was destined to follow Nixon.

He also had to turn down two ambitious junior producers from Germany to act in a movie tentatively titled *The NeverEnding Story of Adolf H.* "Play our Führer!" Balder and Mario asked him. Horsey had a secret meeting with them and the proposed director Helen Bertha who told him about Hitler's eyes: "Hitler's face was all eyes. His blue eyes paralyzed thinking. They were like stars. Like yours."

Horsey's eyes were shining as if freshly cleaned. Helen Bertha was fascinated.

"The Führer moved precisely like a clockwork. As if he had been a product from Henry Ford's assembly line. Like a robot. Immortal and indestructible. Truly the Man of Steel! Man of the Future!!"

"Present. Man of Steel. Man of the Future, too, Ma'am."

Horsey stood up and went for a short stroll. He walked exactly like a robot.

"I would feel honored to accept that part," Horsey pondered, "but…"

"But—*what*, Herr Horsey?" Helen Bertha wanted to know.

"I am supposed to evangelize all America and then…"

"?"

"…continue my mission on Mars. I got no time for such a demanding role as that of Herr Hitler."

"But without you we cannot do the project."

"You should have come earlier. When my pal Rio was still alive. He was the best Jewish Hitler ever."

"A *Jewish* Hitler?"

"Yeah, we don't mind. He was great in that part. But they had to shoot him when he was going to assassinate Von. It's a big loss for TV."

As some had already expected, Mario and Balder's film project fell apart and with it, Helen Bertha's comeback to the silver screen. Shortly after, Mario and Balder had a break-off. Between them it was like East and West Germany. Each decided to do his own Hitler movie and surpass the other.

But the conversation with Helen Bertha was not lost on Horsey. Horsey was going to use those Hitler eyes. He was determined to take off where Nixon had crash-landed. Anyway, Nixon got people only to the Moon. He would bring them to conquer the universe. And beyond.

19 Star-Spangled Eyes

IT WAS VERY COLD that morning. But Horsey wore no coat. He left the impression that he was the proverbial Man of Steel when he delivered his Inaugural Speech at the West Front of the Capitol, his gaze steadfast into the TV camera mesmerizing millions of Americans. Now he wasn't second fiddle to John Wayne. Nixon and Watergate had become a speck of bird poop that was otherwise outshined by a glorious history. Now *he* was America's Number One Star. Thanks to his acting skills and his photographic, i.e., robotic memory, he was as great in front of the cameras as Hitler was:

It is time for us to realize that we're too great a nation to limit ourselves to small dreams. We're not, as some would have us believe, doomed to an inevitable decline. I do not believe in a fate that will fall on us no matter what we do. I do believe in a fate that will fall on us if we do nothing. So, with all the creative energy at our command, let us begin an era of national renewal. Let us renew our determination, our courage, and our strength. And let us renew our faith and our hope.

We have every right to dream heroic dreams. Those who say that we're in a time when there are no heroes, they just don't know where to look. You can see heroes every day going in and out of fac-

tory gates. Others, a handful in number, produce enough food to feed all of us and then the world beyond. You meet heroes across a counter, and they're on both sides of that counter. There are entre-preneurs with faith in themselves and faith in an idea who create new jobs and new wealth, make our economy grow beyond belief. Their patriotism is quiet, but deep. Their values sustain our na-tional life.

Now, I have used the words "they" and "their" in speaking of these heroes. I could say "you" and "your"—because I'm addressing the heroes of whom I speak…

Horsey raised his voice,

– *YOU, the citizens of this blessed country. Your dreams, your hopes, your goals are going to be the dreams, the hopes, and the goals of this administration, so help me God.*

We shall reflect the compassion that is so much a part of your make-up.

While he delivered his sermon, he let his eyes wander around: searching for familiar faces. There were some supporters, mem-bers of the Distler Organization, Old Man Trapp and his ill-man-nered son Mickey, that pain in the ass. But there was no Hitler. No more the phantom ghost of Rio that dressed and was made up as the Führer.

Horsey repressed the memory and took a deep breath. The curse for the betrayal of a friend was finally taken off him.

Rio was dead. Homer. Even Distler was withdrawn from cir-culation and declared dead.

And let me make that one promise, Horsey continued. And as Mars was still fresh in his mind, his hand pointed sky-high.

Recently, the Pope, a faithful man from Poland, a sworn enemy to Communism, has said that he would baptize Martians. Who are we to close doors? My great, late mentor Von, the pioneer of Ameri-can spaceflight, had guided us in the right direction. Up to the stars. Who is going to conquer the universe, will have all right to smash the Kingdom of Evil on Earth!

Applause! Applause!! Applause!!!

Yes, let us pray for the salvation of all of those who live in that totalitarian darkness.

What if free people could live secure in the knowledge that their security did not rest upon the threat of instant U.S. retaliation to deter a Soviet attack, that we could intercept and destroy strategic ballistic missiles before they reached our own soil or that of our allies? I call upon the scientific community in our country, those who gave us nuclear weapons, to turn their great talents now to the cause of mankind and world peace, to give us the means of rendering these nuclear weapons impotent and obsolete.

Joy's gown cost $25,000, a lot of money in those days. Her ambition was to outdo Jackie Kennedy and re-create Camelot twice as big at the White House.

The first thing Horsey asked his Chief of Staff to see was the War Room. Obviously, he had seen it in a Stanley Kubrick movie, but there was no such thing. One could see that Horsey was disappointed, "We better have a War Room."

Only Horsey's (adopted) daughter Perri (named after a true-life adventure of Distler's film factory) turned out a black sheep: On the day of the Inauguration, she appeared nude on the cover of *Playboy* magazine. She sympathized with the Hippie movement and had some of them invited to the White House. Horsey and Joy were shocked when they saw these people smoking pot in the Oval Office. *Make Love, Not War!* was their slogan.

Horsey was determined to show it to them: *Make War, Not Love!*

Schnitzel ordered him to immediately sign a National Security Decision Directive, which included a "vigorous research and development program on ballistic missile defense systems".

"Yeah, let's get a Death Star ®."

Horsey invited Georg Lukas and his dream smiths to the White House.

The Death Star®, as all *Stars of War* fans will know, was a gargantuan space station armed, a colossal weapon the size of the Moon with a planet-destroying *super*laser powered by massive kyber crystals.

Horsey agreed that anything that was called *super* would be good for America.

According to Lukas, the *super*laser was a triumph of combat engineering. Eight individual laser stations produced beams of super-charged energy which converged at an amplification nexus in front of the massive focus lens. This lens, built around an amplification crystal, combined and amplified the eight separate beams into a single *super*laser beam with enough power to shatter a planet.

"Will it be able to shatter the Soviet Union too? I mean: just a friendly threatening gesture."

"Why not? We could turn the idea into a strategic defense initiative movie…"

"Sounds great, Mr. Lukas: Strategic defense initiative."

Lukas had brought not only blueprints. He also placed an actual model of the Death Star ® on Horsey's desk at the Oval Office.

"You mean we only need to introduce it in a…"

"…propaganda documentary produced by Georglukasfilm Ltd. Propaganda for the good cause, for the…"

"Star-Spangled Banner."

Horsey's inner voice had told him that such a Strategic Defense Initiative complete with the imaginary but widely tooted threat of a Death Star ® might be most effective as a propaganda tool to put military and economic pressure on the Soviet Union to fund, in defense, their own outer space missile system and, as a result, declare bankruptcy.

Upon leaving, the Georglukasfilm people encountered Hubbell and his Church of Joy entourage. Hubbell was a regular guest to the White House where he occasionally would share the bedroom with Joy and her astrologer. From time to time, they made world policy in bed.

A few months later Horsey officially visited the City of West Berlin and, with a nod to the Iron Curtain of the Berlin Gate, asked,

"Why is the wall there? We don't need it! There is one sign the Soviets can make that would be unmistakable, that would advance dramatically the cause of freedom and peace. General Secretary Gorbachev, if you seek peace, if you seek prosperity for the Soviet Union and Eastern Europe, if you seek liberalization, come here to this gate, Mr. Gorbachev. Mr. Gorbachev, open this gate. Mr. Gorbachev, tear down this wall!"

Horsey's last words, however, went unheard in the tumultuous, crazy applause that broke out.

Here are these words. The Soviet listeners understood them well:

"For if you don't, we will have the ultimate weapon to destroy it! And destroy you!!"

20 German in the Blood

A FEW YEARS LATER, the Wall opened indeed thanks to Horsey's *Stars at War* Initiative and the threat of an imaginary Death Ray ® device that seemed to be real.

Mario Montini who had split up with Balder Deich was still trying to cast his version of Hitler's life. He wasn't willing to give up the idea. The same was true for Balder. At that time, he was based in a small office at Mussolini's Cinecittà Studios in Rome where he was said to have been involved in money laundering for the Mafia. Each week he announced a new name to play the Führer: George Clooney. Sean Connery. Tom Cruise. Jerry Lewis. Even Richard Pryor although he wasn't qualified for the job: Richard was Afro-American and his mother a prostitute. That wouldn't fit the bill. Definitely not. Finally, Mario settled for Udo Kier. But then he had a stroke and lost his speech, and Deich made the race recalling the last ten days in the Führer Bunker like the fatal end of the Teutonic epic dealing with *Nibelung loyalty*.

Deich in an interview: *It is much more than a gloomy chapter. It is the most dramatic part of German history and as that something that concerns us all. My parents have experienced the war. I myself was born right after the war and have experienced vividly the effects. So I began to busy myself with the German history and especially NS history. For 20 years, I'm doing intense reading on this period.*

Another book by the author of the controversial Hitler biography, Joachim C. Fest, provided the source material the movie *Doom & Wreck* was based on that became Deich's guideline: *Fest, so to speak, handed me the dramaturgic key to write the screenplay. In the book he not only observes the final days of Hitler but the collapse of the whole system. In these twelve days one could observe all the mechanisms of the NS regime as if in a nutshell, and this in an intensified form because events at the end of the war did dramatize once more.*

Deich called the project his greatest challenge (since then everything was turned into a challenge):

To do what no one has dared since: to portray the personalities who have shaped the NS regime in great parts as three-dimensional characters. And with it break with previous demonization and break a taboo. The objective was not to deliver a template but to penetrate the personalities. And win insights which, I guess, are very important.

One shouldn't regard the evil as an abstract mass which takes on a life of its own and then affects the people but should understand that these are people who have their own emotions with whom people can identify in case of doubt to a certain degree.

Deich, who was quite simple-minded, a Karl May (same as Hitler) and comics devotee and personal friend of Marvel's Stan Lee (he had invested some millions of other people's money in one of Lee's properties), wanted to show *Hitler the human*. He began his film treatment not in the bunker in 1945 but with the introduction of a young lady who applies for a job as Hitler's secretary at Wolfsschanze, the Führer's command post Wolf's Lair in the Masurian woods. Traudl Junge is pretty nervous and in a typewriting test makes many mistakes but Hitler consoles her because he likes that girl from Munich: a nice, grandfatherly gentleman, not evil at all, revealing the human touch of the monster: the fatalism of evil. As a German, you sure would like to become his friend.

...if the film has one value, Deich said, *it is the fact that it contains no judgement.* No judgement concerning the crimes: Sympathy for the Devil—to quote the Rolling Stones. The lesson is clear: Hitler was no beast but was "the best".

The holocaust didn't fit in the whitewashed image of this Film-*Ver*-*"Führer"* (seducer) and was referred to only briefly, as sort of an accident at work. Otherwise, the dictator was portrayed as a soft-spoken dreamer with a human side who enjoys pasta and chocolate cake: no antihero, a negative hero but a **hero** anyway.

The production was to mark Helen Bertha's triumphant return to Hollywood, to a place that, thanks to Georglukasfilm's blockbusters resembled more and more a Norse Valhalla.

Contrary to the days of David Selznick, Louis B. Mayer, Harry Cohn or Darryl Zanuck, the place was run now by ambitious young lawyers who were not interested in the product (a wave of sequels, anyway) but in the stock market. Hitler, Mister Spock or Luke Skywalker—to them it didn't matter.

They only objected Helen Bertha. Yes, Helen Bertha was still alive. She even did scuba diving and underwater photography. But although she was fit as a fiddle, the lawyers considered her way too old now to entertain the kids of the popcorn generation. Instead, she was introduced by Balder Deich as patroness—whatever that title meant, holding a welcome glass of champagne. Then Balder said that to him such an important movie like that of the final days of our Führer could be competently made only in Hollywood and only with an American director in charge:

"Our movie will be as spectacular as *Stars at War, The Alamo,* and *Ragnarok* together and will combine elements of all three." Cocaine had left a visible effect on the mind and the gigantomania of Balder Deich.

"Who is going to play your Führer?"

"There is going to be a race between the best actors Hollywood has to offer. Like in the good old days of *Gone with the Wind.*"

When she heard that title mentioned, Helen Bertha exploded, "They denied me the part of Scarlett, you know, those Jewish bastards."

They shut her up with another glass of champagne.

This time Horsey, the retired President of the United States, was out of question for the job. Officially, he had become a victim of Alzheimer's disease. In fact, Horsey's batteries were running out. Joy and the Church of Joy, with the backing of the Distler Organization, blocked him off from the public.

"I now begin the journey that will lead me into the sunset of my life."

Hitler's mind and eyes that once took possession of him like a virus had left him in a state of mental darkness—ready to find another host, somebody who had more German in the blood.

Horsey just sat there in his chair and dozed. Sometimes he looked up to the nightly sky and hoped that Von would appear and deliver on his promise: to get him to Mars!

Of all people it was Hubbell who felt pity for the worn-out man and took him to a studio tour at Paramount. At one soundstage they were busy shooting a sci-fi movie based on a script by the founder of that new Space Religion that undermined Hollywood. Tom, Will and John were cast as Martians and posed for photos with Horsey. One of the guys, a bodybuilder named Arnold Strong, was particularly pushy. He was from Styria, the second largest state of Austria, and talked insistently to Horsey who didn't understand a word. Arnold felt that he should be a politician too, someday, and wanted to know Horsey's corporate secret. Then he told him that he was dating a girl who knew Horsey well.

Horsey looked at him.

"Doris."

"Doris?"

"Yes, Doris. Doris Todt. She was in one of your TV shows in the 1950s. Pretty young then."

"Doris," the ex-president mumbled. "Doris… Death."

"Not Death, Mr. President. Just—Todt."

Anyway, the former President was seen in the company of Martians or at least people who looked that way, google-eyed, with antennae on their head.

Then, all of a sudden, he stood in front of Hitler!

Hitler was very cordial and invited him over to the studio canteen, "Today they'll have Schnitzel."

"Schnitzel?"

"Ja."

"But I can't eat meat anymore, Rio. My teeth are failing."

Then he fell asleep and was escorted back to his chauffeur-driven car.

The character who had invited Horsey to join him on a walk to the studio canteen was neither Rio nor Hitler. He was merely a character actor who just was cast by Balder's company who occupied an adjacent stage on the Paramount lot.

From then on, the Space Monsters from Hubbell's set were regular guests of the Führer and Helen Bertha and they mixed with each other.

To Helen Bertha who messed with everything the Monsters looked like Nuba warriors. The Nuba were a cluster of African tribes she had visited and photographed in the late 1960s. These photographs had confirmed the old lady's reputation as an unrepentant Nazi. "You know, 20,000 Nuba were singing and dancing for me when I arrived there," Helen Bertha exaggerated while her eyes critically checked the Space Monsters' balls. "Naked, in the buff." She even suggested to add a dream sequence, a nightmare that took hold of the Führer's mind: introducing Russian devils that looked like Space Monster Nuba. The sequence was never shot.

A short time before the release of Balder's film, Mel Gibson's *The Passion of Christ* had hit the cinemas like one of Von's V-2 rockets. Now Balder had produced sort of *The Passion of Adolf Hitler*.

Gruesome? Grotesque? Shocking? Sickening?

None of these descriptions fully captured the movie's portrayal of the suffering of Adolf Hitler as seen by Balder, the nephew of "Uncle" Albin. Only the most unfeeling individual could have watched this film and not felt pity for poor Adolf. The faces of (gentile, non-Jewish) cinemagoers expressed somberness, fright and shock—just to name a few emotions. Some even had tears in their eyes. If the mission of this movie was to evoke emotion, producer Balder Deich deserved an A+.

But Deich couldn't enjoy his success anymore. When the movie was finished and distributed all over America by Buena Noche, Distler's Releasing Company, Balder Deich was dead. Right before the Hollywood premiere on April 30, his boyish wish to go and see Distlerland and the shrine with the original Skull Ring came true.

"You're hungry, Balder?" Distler's lawyers asked.

"Well, I would like to have a bite."

"We have a great restaurant here. Very German. You will like it. Be our guest."

The lawyers led him to Trapp's Schnitzel Restaurant on the lot.

And when the meal was served on a large plate, perfect to the tiniest detail, Balder's head fell right into the XXL cutlet.

Heart attack.

The Passion of Adolf Hitler was Balder's last will. And Albin's as well. The fatalism of evil was what prevailed in the poisoned minds of the spectators.

Horsey didn't see it. What he saw was a *Making of* on TV.

He saw it in the company of Rio and his favorite Martian who visited his decaying mind now on a regular basis.

Joy, in the meantime, earned a bit extra and loaned her smile to the Church of Joy.

21 Teutonic Woodstock on the Night of the Witches

THE MAN, who was to become Horsey's legitimate disciple, one who had more German in his blood than most people he knew, was a member of the Trapp Family. The man's name was— *Mickey*!

Now he was waiting for his baptism of fire. That meant he had to make a trip to the country of his ancestors.

A reason had to be found to spill blood, no Halloween fake blood; no, the real red lifeblood: unrestrained. Roughly 14 kilometers southwest from the cathedral city Paderborn, in the black forests of Germany, there towered a castle well-known to all occultists and well-known to neo-Nazis. We have heard of it: Wewelsburg. This place was an ideal object for a flaming beacon that was destined to become Mickey's *Feuerprobe*, Mickey's ordeal.

April 30 held a special meaning for people who knew the secrets of the occult and the secrets of Nazism which went synonymous. On April 30, 1945, known in vulgar superstition as Walpurgis Night or Witches' Sabbath, the same day Lord Haw-Haw a.k.a. Nazi Propagandist William Joyce called for crusade against the victorious Bolsheviks, Adolf Hitler, and his newlywed bride Eva née Braun were said to have committed suicide in the vast bunker complex of the Reich Chancellery in Berlin to ride with other devil-worshippers home to Blocksberg. In the interim, all plans for a New World Order had been buried. But only in the interim. Of course, now we know that Hitler's eyes and mind did survive and lived on.

Hallervorden, Ziska and Todt were present to save his brain and put it in a black box. The freight was to be shipped to Hollywood. Walpurgis Night, April 30, 1945, was the *Night the Nazis Invaded Hollywood.* Of the three scientists who knew the secret only Todt was supposed to act as the guardian, to handle the shipping, a slave of Hitler's brain.

There were many April 30s, past and present.

On April 30, 1315, French chamberlain Enguerrand de Marigny was hanged on the public gallows at Montfaucon after being convicted of sorcery.

April 30, 1349: The Jewish community of Radolfzell at Lake Constance was exterminated.

April 30, 1492: Spain announced that it would expel all Jews.

April 30, 1563: Jews were expelled from France by order of Charles VI.

April 30, 1763: John Wilkes, Member of Parliament and journalist, charged with seditious libel and confined in the Tower of London.

April 30, 1789: George Washington was inaugurated as the first President of the United States of America.

April 30, 1900: An unlucky day for Casey Jones who died in a train wreck at Vaughn, Mississippi, while driving the Cannonball Express.

April 30, 1938: German Comedian Fips Asmussen born in Hamburg.

April 30, 1943: The Bergen-Belsen Concentration Camp for Jews.

April 30, 1948: U.S. performed a nuclear test at Enwetak.

April 30, 1952: Mr. Potato Head, the first toy advertised on TV.

April 30, 1966: At the Black House in San Francisco Anton Szandor LaVey, born Howard Stanton Levey, ritualistically shaved his head and, influenced by Friedrich Nietzsche, Ayn Rand, Aleister Crowley, H. L. Mencken and the writers of *Weird Tales* pulp fiction, declared the Church of Satan to be established to rival the Church of Joy.

April 30, 1968: Verona Pooth née Feldbusch born in La Paz, Bolivia.

April 30, 1970: U.S. troops invaded Cambodia.

The same day actress Inger Stevens died from acute barbiturate poisoning, most likely suicide.

April 30, 1974: Richard Nixon handed over partial transcripts of the Watergate tape recordings.

April 30, 1975: The forces of the Viet Cong gained control of Saigon.

April 30, 1982: Kirsten Dunst born in Point Pleasant, New Jersey.

April 30, 1985: France performed nuclear test at Mururoa atoll.

April 30, 1992: The final episode of *The Bill Cosby Show* on NBC-TV.

April 30, 1993: The World Wide Web source code released by CERN, thus making the software freely available to the general public.

April 30, 1997: Big Ben stopped at 12:11 p.m. for 54 minutes.

April 30, 2008: Heidi Klum, Germany's Next Top Model, launched her clothing line for Jordache.

April 30, 2009: Chrysler automobile company filed for Chapter 11 bankruptcy.

April 30, 2012: Overloaded ferry killing 103 people in the Brahmaputra River in India.

April 30, 2013: 13 people killed after bomb explosion in Damascus.

April 30, 2018: World's oldest known spider, a female trapdoor, aged 43, died being killed by a wasp sting in Western Australia.

Not to forget Danish filmmaker Lars "von" Trier. He was born April 30, 1956 in Copenhagen. Trier was one to brainwash himself and later brainwashing others. In 2011, at the Cannes Film Festival, asked if his Germanic roots influenced his work, the unpredictable filmmaker demonstrated sympathy for the Devil, "The only thing I can tell you is that I thought I was a Jew for a long time and was very happy being a Jew, then later on came [Danish and Jewish director] Susanne Bier, and suddenly I wasn't so happy about being a Jew. That was a joke. Sorry. But it turned out that I was not a Jew. If I'd been a Jew, then I would have been a second-wave Jew, a kind of a new-wave Jew, but anyway, I really wanted to be a Jew and then I found out that I was really a Nazi. Because my family was German... which also gave me some pleasure. So I'm kind of a... What can I say? *I understand Hitler.* But I think he did some wrong things, yes, absolutely, but I can see him sitting in his bunker. But there will come a point, at the end of this... I'm just saying, I think I understand the man. He's not what you call a good guy, but yeah, I understand much about him and I sympathize with him a little bit. But come on, I'm not for the Second World War, and I'm not against Jews... I am of course very much for Jews. No, not too much, because Israel is a pain in the ass. But still, how can I get out of this sentence? No, I just want to say about the art, I'm very much for Speer. Albert Speer, I liked. He was also maybe one of God's best children. He had some talent that was kind of possible for him to use... OKAY, I'M A NAZI."

Trier must have been drunk talking such nonsense.

Later, at a retrospective of his work in Berlin, Trier put even more coal on the fire, "I think history shows that we are all Nazis somewhere, and there are a lot of things that can be suddenly set free, and the mechanics behind this setting-free is something we really should investigate, and the way we do not investigate it is to make it a taboo to talk about it." (Consequently, "von" Trier's movie *Antichrist* was co-funded with lots of German state money, thanks to Filmstiftung North Rhine-Westphalia in Düsseldorf.)

April 30 was certainly a black day.

The timing was great for Mickey to experience April 30 in Germany. Mickey, planning his Mystery Road trip through Europe, was wondering "if anyone knows about some funky places to visit. All spots are welcome, from ghost towns to UFO hotspots or whatever funkiness you know about." The suggestions he received from German sources, besides Blocksberg a.k.a. Brocken, included Externsteine, a rocky center of religious Teutonic activity, vastly researched by the SS, and the SS Ordensburg Wewelsburg Castle where Himmler's cohorts gathered under the Black Sun and prepared for the expected big conflict between Europe and the rest of the world. He remembered that his Dad once told him that a distant relative named Albin was ordained in that castle. Therefore, in a way, he considered Wewelsburg Castle a power source of his ancestors. He simply had to go and see the place with his own eyes: being baptized by the Spirits of this Power.

On Friday, November 3, 1933, in the presence of Freiherr von Oeynhausen und Ballenstedt, Reichsführer SS Heinrich Himmler had seen the castle for the first time. Between him and the building it was a *coup de foudre*, it was like love at first sight. He decided to buy the place here and now. Initially intended as a "Reichsführer School" for SS officers, measures were taken at the end of the 1930s to restore the place and progressively transform the Castle into a secluded, occult shrine for the highest-ranking SS officers complete with religious services of swearing-in ceremonies: the New Ordensburg of the Nazis' Round Table, the future center of the Earth.

Buried in the depths inside the Castle were the roots of Yggdrasil, the mighty tree of Norse mythology. When the tree trembles, the legend goes, it signals the arrival of Ragnarok, the destruction of the universe.

There even was an occult black metal band by that name, Ragnarok, appearing on stage near the Castle the very day, April 30, Mickey came to visit and receive the gift of a *Third Eye*, considered to be the organ of supreme universal collection. The German neo-Nazis who organized the event were determined to transform the *Wewelsburg concert* into an unforgettable rally that outshined Woodstock. Young Nazi filmmakers were around to record that memorable day. Special effects and explosives were secretly prepared to make it really unforgettable.

When Mickey was about to leave the Castle, he heard them calling outside: *Flamme empor!—Flame up!*

Mickey thought it would be better to return to the hotel, but then a voice told him to stay until nightfall. It was the voice of a female.

She looked gorgeous.

She reminded him of Rita Hayworth. Green hunting suit. Black boots.

Mickey looked at her with wide eyes.

She might have been 17 or 18, much younger than he was.

She laughed, "Heute ist Walpurgisnacht."

"Sorry, I don't understand. I'm American."

"Oh, you're from America." She changed the conversation from German to English.

"Today is Walpurgis Night. Witches' Sabbath."

"I know."

"You look like Rita Hayworth. My name is Mickey. What's yours?"

"I'm… Rita."

"Damned. You could be her daughter."

"Are you looking for an experience, American?"

"To a certain extent, yes."

"Then come with me. I have something for you."

Mickey couldn't resist the temptation.

They walked for a while, then entered a cottage.

"You live in this?"

"Just so."

She threw him a can with a special ointment, also known as flying ointment, green ointment, magic salve and lycanthropic ointment.

"We're gonna ride tonight! Put on the lotion. It will help us… get up."

"Get up?"

"Don't ask. Put on the lotion."

She buttoned up his shirt and put on the lotion.

The ointment worked like a drug, like LSD or ACID. The effect was hallucinogenic.

Everything in front of Mickey's eyes was blurred.

"Come! Come here!"

Rita offered him a jar, "Drink!"

Mickey gulped.

Then she pulled his hands on her breasts.

And while he did so, he began to float, outside the cottage, high and higher.

April 30. Saint Walpurga's Eve!

An eerie atmosphere. Everywhere fires.

Wraithlike, in pale moonlight: witches and sorcerers riding on broomsticks, pitchforks, baking trays, flying goats, cats, pigs.

They were heading for Wewelsburg.

While the Hippies in America flew over the cuckoo's nest, Mickey flew over German history.

High above Wewelsburg Castle.

Down there they saw dark creatures with torches. Seven circles of dancers had transformed into a spiral.

They heard loud music, saw mercenary soldiers and members of military-sports-group *Tyr* set Wewelsburg afire. A Skinhead gathering of shaved heads, black bomber jackets, combat boots and swastika tattoos.

The names of the Black Metal bands that played were *Endlösung: Final Solution* and *Gaskammer: Gas Chamber.*

In front of Mickey's *Third Eye* the flames shot up and illuminated the nightly sky.

In the background the mastermind of the explosive show.

"See," Rita screamed against the wind, "there's HIM!"

"Who is it?"

"He's the Master. We call him Satan."

"Oh, you mean the guy who was behind *The Exorcist*? That was a great movie, wasn't it?"

He saw Satan raising his fist in the air. Illuminated by the fires, his shape seemed glittering gold. His glance dazzled. He wore an Original Halloween Michael Myers mask manufactured by Don Post Studios.

Mickey looked bashfully to the ground.

The Satan figure was surrounded by a whole bunch of Goth girls clothed in black leather.

He heard them yell, "*All or nothing! ALL OR NOTHING!!*"

The neo-Nazis were going to finish the job that a demolition squad of the SS had attempted in 1945: to blow up the triangular castle. They failed but the fire had destroyed huge parts of the building. Now what had remained should burn to the ground too.

Fire sirens woke him up from trance. It was a hell of a spectacle.

Mickey looked around. Rita was gone. There were only policemen. They eyed him suspiciously and asked to see his ID card.

The fire at Wewelsburg was extinguished.

Satan and members of his group that hadn't escaped were arrested and led away in handcuffs.

22 The Black Steam Iron Murders

HUMOR HADN'T SEEN a TV set for half a century. Due to ill-advised business dealings on the part of Roach's son and bankruptcy, Hal Roach Studios had been closed in April 1959 with the lot demolished in August 1963.

Humor was older than dirt but welcomed the opportunity to return and lend his skills to a series of mayhem and murder.

During his German trip Mickey had not only had his baptism of fire, the experience of the flaming torch, and the alleged gift of the *Third Eye*. He also had seen an inspiring German TV show that became the blueprint for his own appearance on TV.

In October 1967, German TV had started a long-running series *Aktenzeichen XY... ungelöst* (*Case number XY... Unsolved*) hosted by Eduard Zimmermann. The goal was to throw light on unsolved crimes with the aid of the viewers who were asked to phone their information and get the criminal a fair trial.

Mickey considered this a brilliant idea although there could have been a little bit more bloodshed. Since Auschwitz, Mickey thought, the Germans were a little reluctant and overcautious concerning this matter. OK, he would change that in his own version that became one of American TV's hit shows: *The Black Steam Iron Murders* were destined to make lynch law popular again (as in the "good old days" when the Nation was born). The original Steam Iron Murderer was supposed to be an Afro-American who brutally killed his victims, preferably white women, with a massive steam iron. Hence the odd title.

The character was absolute fiction but presented in a way that he became an *authentic* horror ghoul, a Boogeyman of sorts that lurked behind every second corner. So, Dad, better lock up your daughter when the autumn moon is bright! Mickey called him, off the record (of course!), the "Nigger that Laid Golden Eggs".

Yes, our Mickey hadn't forgotten the way Horsey climbed the ladder. While Horsey had promoted Von and the Moon landing, Mickey would enter Reality TV with a format adopted from the Germans (who else!), with the added bonus of a merchandise concept that included T-shirts and Halloween with the Black Boogeyman's face on it, and guns, guns, guns with Mickey's portrait engraved.

The message went: *America, arm yourself!* Mickey joined forces with the American arms industry that came forward to sponsor the show. In the trade papers, he presented himself by holding a rifle, like Horsey in the early days of his career. He expanded the concept of the Germans considerably: He asked his viewers not only to phone but to bring the perpetrators—*dead or alive*. Best, get them to the next gallows as soon as possible.

It was self-evident that Mickey, for the sake of quotas, would not only choose (and sometimes invent) the bloodiest murder cases but would hype them by hiring some horror film directors from Hollywood and abroad to illustrate the respective cases with video clips. It was all sex & mayhem! Believe it or else, he even was going to contact David Lynch because his name fit in splendidly with the hoped-for lynch law. Lynch turned him down. Others, mostly cheap exploitation guys, welcomed the chance of an additional income. Russ Meyer of *Supervixens* fame was approached and said that he wouldn't mind provided the money was right but had a slight disagreement with Mickey who grabbed Meyer's "biggest tits" for himself.

One day Mickey was about to buy some property from a real estate broker. The man's name was Al Adamson.

"Adamson? Adamson? Aren't you *the* Adamson who made *Psycho-A-Go-Go*?"

Al Adamson grinned from ear to ear and was all smiles. He once was really one of those unsung Schlock masters. Mickey had seen and admired Al's crime thriller *Psycho-A-Go-Go* when he was ready to go to Vietnam. He called it one of the most underrated movies of all time. For all who don't know, this version of *Psycho* was about a psychotic jewel thief named Joe Corey who stalked a young woman and her child into the wilderness. Adamson was none to waste his stuff. A few years later, in 1969, he took the film and re-edited it into *The Fiend with the Electronic Brain* with the added attraction of John Carradine as mad scientist. Still dissatisfied, in 1971 he cut the whole thing into *Blood of Ghastly Horror*. Ade Brunner in Germany couldn't have done it any better.

Al had done more trash like *Satan's Sadists, The Female Bunch, Angel's Wild Women, The Dynamite Brothers, The Naughty Stewardesses,* and *Sex 2000* (that circulated in Germany under the title *Liebe im Raumschiff Venus = Love in Spaceship Venus*).

"But why did my movies save you from going to Vietnam?" Al wanted to know.

"I saw your masterpiece in some drive-in theater, and when I left the show with my car, I had an accident. So I couldn't possibly go."

"Were you seriously hurt?"

"Not physically, but the shock, the SHOCK… I still feel it… first your movie, then the accident."

"I understand."

"I simply couldn't go to Vietnam. But my Dad contributed some money to the war effort. And now that my life was spared by not going to Vietnam, I pay my tribute to this country even more so—by calling out a purging crusade."

Al was Mickey's man and acted as gore consultant—until he was murdered himself. Not by the Black Boogeyman but by a live-in contractor whom he had hired to work on his house. Al's corpse was found buried beneath his floor.

Mickey had to do without him but in the meantime had learned enough from the masters of schlock to handle the task of directing his Horror Picture Shows himself.

He fell in love with every second starlet that played a female victim in his show. Usually, these were one-night stands. But then came Rita. Yes, the witch he had met at Wewelsburg Castle. She had returned to him with the clear ambition to become a top model. The Trapp Production Company immediately signed the aspiring starlet as regular victim for *Black Steam Iron Murders*. Gosh, her red hair bathed in red blood! These awesome colors!

Rita didn't speak fluent English. So she was told to keep her mouth shut and only groaned when she was raped and killed in the show. She certainly knew how to twist Mickey around her little finger. Each time they went to bed she asked Mickey for a present, little gems, expensive clothes, exquisite perfumes. Sometimes a cheque would do so that Rita could go to a boutique herself.

One night, Mickey popped the question to her. He couldn't hold the words back. He was too drunk. The words spluttered uncontrollably out of his mouth. And Rita said *Ja!—Yes*!

But while he kissed her, Mickey had already other women in mind.

That contributed to his downfall the moment he seemed to have reached his peak determined to run for President of the United States.

23 A Road Map of How To Become the Next President of the United States of America

BUT MICKEY HAD a serious rival—on Reality TV as well as in the Republican Party presidential primaries and caucuses. His name was Donald. Donald was as ruthless and loudmouthed as Mickey. He had never read a history book but now had decided to be written about not only in manager and playboy magazines but in expensive, leather-bound history books. How could mankind do without him? They need me! They need Me!! But how to get inside such printed volumes? Of course, he could pay his way inside but to a golfer like him that would be unsporting. Sure, he had a book ghostwritten (he didn't even read it, he just had his name above the title): Not *How to Become a Millionaire*, no, no— he topped it with *How to Become a Billionaire*. But what we were talking now were legitimate books: eternal books like the *Bible* that was written or co-written by another God. His sycophants reinforced his megalomania: You haven't read a single page of Tolstoy's *War and Peace*, not even seen the movie, but why only read about it when *You* can become the Master of War and Peace yourself!

These words introduced Donald to a splendid idea: Become not only the Master of War and Peace! Why not go the extra mile and become the Master of Universe?

Neither Mickey nor Donald ever read Orwell. To both of them, 1984 was a bygone period: yesteryear. They never had heard about that Polish scribbler Lem. Nevertheless, instinctively, they both became eager competitors at the keyboard of *Phantomology*.

Half a century ago, Stanisław Lem had a vision about the consequences of what we call today, thoughtlessly: *Virtual Reality*. He termed this vision *Phantomology* which describes a (waking) state in which fiction and reality become indistinguishable.

What can a person, connected to a phantomatic generator, experience? Everything. He can scale mountain cliffs, walk without a space suit or oxygen mask on the surface of the Moon, in a clanking armor he can lead a faithful posse to conquer medieval forts or the North Pole. He can be adulated by crowds as a marathon winner or as the greatest poet of all time and accept the Nobel Prize from the hands of a Swedish King, indulge in the requited love of Mme. Pompadour, duel with Iago to avenge Othello, or get stabbed himself by Mafia hitmen. He can also grow enormous eagle wings and fly; or else become a fish and live his life on the coral reef; as an immense shark he can pursue schools of prey with jaws wide open, more! he can snatch swimming people, chew them up with a gusto and then digest in a tranquil nook of his underwater cavern.

Lem was not that much worried about the technology itself—but about the consequences of deception, the mix of reality and fiction. Where does the vision begin, where does the illusion end? How high will be the level of immersion?

Although this was too much for the simple minds of Donald and Mickey, they knew from experience that the world of the media was a world of make-believe. And according to the laws of

Virtual Reality, *Donald the Upcoming Master of the Universe* was determined to dump *Mickey the Immortal!*

All the time, Mickey had carried a fresh flask with him filled with Rita's lotion that made him fly high above Wewelsburg. All his energy came from these flights into imagination.

When he took a sip, his mind went sky high. He flew straight, all the way from Trapp Headquarters in New York City to Washington, D.C., circling above Capitol and White House that was occupied by a colored man at that time. He told himself that he was the right man to have it cleaned to the last angle.

His twisted mind run amuck, "I am going to disinfect and sterilize the whole country from niggers' smell and Mexican tortillas."

First, he flew together with Rita as his "co-pilot", but then his playboy mind invited other women to share the ointment with.

And while he flew those girls above Washington's landmarks, he saw a huge swastika down there in the Lincoln Memorial Reflecting Pool.

In the meantime, the Trapp Empire had run into business problems and declared, for various companies, bankruptcy a dozen times. Mickey survived because he knew legal spider holes and even generated money from that. More serious, however, he was suspected of tax fraud, money laundry, and bribery, obviously a Trapp family tradition.

Rita was jealous. Mickey had promised to marry her but the date of the wedding was delayed and delayed and delayed—until Rita knew for sure that Mickey the Womanizer wouldn't keep his promise. She disliked the prospect of fading away. She knew he wouldn't make her First Lady, so she'd better destroy him.

Like Mickey, Donald had no program, just a single phrase he already used while still a teenager yanking Doris's pigtails: *Make America Great Again! Make America Great Again!! Make America Great Again!!!* He repeated the phrase like a mantra, and it got caught on in the minds of the stupid and needless who were supposed to elect him: the disadvantaged, slaughter cattle in its own right.

Donald admired and envied strong leaders like Xi Jinping, Vladimir Putin, and Kim Jong-un because they were no subjects of democratic legislative periods.

There were a lot of other personalities to learn from too: Adolf Hitler, the Joker and Darth Vader included! Donald didn't wish upon a star. He wished upon a Death Star ®. In his eyes this was more explosive.

Yeah, Master of War and Peace! Master of Life and Death!! Master of Universe!!!

You will be the string-puller: Let the puppets dance! Of course, he was not aware that he was a marionette himself but Donald had definitely set his mind on getting elected President of the United States: triumphing over Mickey.

The only way to accomplish the mission was to knock on the door of the Distler Organization. Quite recently, Distler had purchased for a couple billion dollars the *Stars at War* franchise and the complete menagerie of America's comic superheroes: Captain Miraculous, Super Sonicman, Spider Woman, The Bulk, The Ant Guy, Wotan the Wonderful, Mr. Spook, and Übermensch.

But Distler was still with Mickey.

Two of Distler's leading producers had become Mickey's election campaign managers. Together they would infiltrate the internet and line up the superheroes as campaign volunteers.

The timing was great for Rita. She and Donald arrived at an agreement. Rita was going to sabotage Mickey's efforts and badmouth him.

The next time Donald flew over the White House he crashed and found himself on the ground in front of the White House, filled with drugs.

The ointment Rita had given him didn't work anymore.

The story of a drug-addicted Mickey made the headlines. Distler had no other choice than to drop this man like a hot potato and transfer his Superheroic campaigners to Donald's service.

Now they thwacked, whooped and peppered each other for the benefit of Donald's victory.

The night Donald had won, he left the Republican party early and just sat for himself: drunk as a skunk, and watched World Wrestling Entertainment on TV. "I will rule this country with the iron grip of a wrestler! I will show those bastards in Washington!! I am going to grill and mince them!!!" But he didn't know what to show them—but anyway: put them through the wringer. The louder you shout... He was a defiant guy.

Suddenly he got hungry and asked Übermensch, who had been promoted out of the pages of Distler's comic books to lead Donald's Praetorian Guard, to get him a *schnitzel*! The Praetorians were loyal Distler robots who would saw the seed of fear. Donald liked when people feared him, the supreme Master.

And while he devoured his *schnitzel* with ravenous appetite, his brain was connected like that of the others and he received a message what to do next. And on and on.

He would lie in bed with a cheeseburger and a young woman, eat, watch the dozen screens around him, news and Distler's ongoing superhero serials, and phone with one of his billionaire friends or one ultra-right-wing conspiracy propagator.

Donald judged people according to the suits they wore: cheaply dressed—bad, expensively dressed—good, uniform—even better.

He didn't like eloquent people. He was to be the main speaker, nobody else. Usually, he asked people to get him something great, "We need something great!!!"

He hated expert knowledge. To him, this was a leftist virtue.

Donald became the most controversial President in the history of the United States and literally cracked the nation.

Then came something great, the pandemic. Donald tried to ignore it, called it the Chinese virus, cursed it—but it caught him flat-footed. Coronavirus SARS-CoV-2 cost him the re-election.

24 Next Exit: Hellgate To Camp Auschwitz

WHAT THE GERMANS can do, I've been able to do for a long time! Mickey might have been forgotten. He might have gone to the dogs but he hadn't forgotten the lesson he had learned while flying high above Wewelsburg Castle!

On January 2021, after their beloved outgoing President had agitated them, Mickey turned up and led the Stormtroopers to the Capitol. They ignored the virus. They had enough virus in their own dumb heads. They even ignored the sanctuaries of American culture.

One of the rioters wore a sweatshirt emblazoned with the phrase "Camp Auschwitz". He was a moron from Virginia. The bottom of the shirt stated, "Work brings freedom", which is the rough translation of the phrase "*Arbeit macht frei*" that was on the concentration camp's gates.

Another conspicuous figure among Mickey's misguided folks wore a so-called Buffalo Cap made of fur and decorated with animal horns. The self-proclaimed "Q-Shaman" had a tattoo of a rune symbol on his bare chest that played with a Nazi symbol and was particularly popular with White Supremacists. He called himself a real patriot who believed in a conspiracy in the highest circles of government, in secret child molestation rings and the ominous, long refuted "pizza connection" that kept making headlines. He found all that bullshit through his own research on the Internet. That research included *Behold a Pale Horse* by the late Arizona author Milton William Copper who had allegedly seen "a flying saucer the size of an aircraft carrier come right out of the ocean and fly into the clouds". The Buffalo-Horned felt immediately illuminated, "At a certain point, it all clicked in a way. I see now the reality of what's going on."

To mindless zombies like him, a shadow world government of Illuminati, Freemasons, and Jews controlled the world.

Indeed, people like him carried a lot of shit in their heads.

At that moment, everybody felt that the Gates of Hell had been opened.

Well, not exactly the Gates of Hell: *the Gates of Human Stupidity*.

Einstein was right when he said, "Two things are infinite: the universe and human stupidity; and I'm not sure about the universe."

By the way, did you know that there was a secret German space program to re-establish bases on Mars during WW2? Zack Schneider, the producer of a documentary titled *The Cosmic Mystery*, claimed that the Nazis (including Thule, Vril, and Black Sun) originally came from Mars but were defeated in fierce territorial battles by the Interplanetary Corporate Conglomerate and had to settle on Earth, in Germany.

The message came too late to reach Horsey. Horsey and Hubbell had passed away some years ago, survived by Horsey's wife Joy and survived by the Church of Joy.

Maybe someday space vehicles jointly funded by NASA and the Distler Organization will return the Nazis to the Red Planet. And maybe one day in the future astronauts will find a new *Schnitzel Factory* right in the Center of Mars.

Among the winners was red-haired Rita.

The money she got from Donald she invested in a company named Brainwaves. When Brainwaves went public, CEO Rita joined with Zanyflix.

The story behind Zanyflix is an entwined one. Zanyflix had become the largest provider of Pay TV series content at a time when the pandemic spread that only accelerated what already was going on: *Zeitenwende,* a turn of eras.

In the series concept of Zanyflix there was no room left for the tradition and values of history: the courage of men, the honor of women, the loving obedience of children. There was only fake, fight, fraught, and murder. *The Black Steam Iron Murders* were nothing against it. There was even no room left for historical truth. Everything became a big mélange. Genghis Khan and Adolf Hitler would meet aboard the Starship Enterprise and talk about the stock market and cryptocurrencies like Bitcoin.

And because global warming and nuclear warfare were said to destroy not just human but *all* life on Earth, Zanyflix transformed the likely disaster into a series. Cashing in by showing doomed man the inevitable future of doom. They were convinced that only a German director could handle the task. His name was Roland Sindelfing. One of Sindelfing's Academy Award-winning films had shown the White House blown to pieces by an armada from outer space. That was a damn break, albeit on screen. Sindelfing, a Swabian through and through, had his crew of German special effects people around to design and film the disaster:

The schedule provided for two takes for each scene that involved explosives. Consequently, two models of the White House were built for each of these scenes, the second as a safety factor.

To capture the explosion from all conceivable angles we installed seven cameras with a frame rate between 300 and 120 frames per second. Except for the main camera, all other angles were planned in a way that no further postprocessing was necessary but that they could be used as plain in-camera effects. The lighting was finished the day before and when all cameras were ready for shooting, everything went by quite fast. The explosion lasted a few seconds and checking the image on the video monitors the result looked quite spectacular so that the whole set could be wrapped the same night.

As a result of that, Sindelfing was asked to contribute his directing skills and his explosive team of Swabian effects experts to a high-budget commercial for a communications company, TeleBridge. At first, they considered a Sindelfing-produced digital version of *Godzilla on the loose*. But then the director had an even better idea, a twist never been used before (if you hadn't seen Jack Gold's *The Medusa Touch*). The spot was supposed to open in a sidewalk cafe in Manhattan.

Sindelfing pitched the idea himself, "Above it, we recognize a skyscraper that resembles, with some imagination, a tower of the World Trade Center. A young couple is served red wine and coffee when the table begins to vibrate. Aircraft engines are roaring. Horrified, the guests look up. They see a passenger airplane crashing in broad daylight into the tower above them. People flee screaming while—cut—the passengers aboard the airplane are given a good shake. The plane penetrates the building like a gigantic arrow and we see a huge billboard with the phone number of the client. No catastrophe, nobody is harmed or injured, no victims, no dead, just a spectacular special effect for entertainment's sake."

"That's great, Roland. How much money do you need?"

Sindelfing smiled. No expenses were spared.

Two days after the broadcast of the finished product Anke Schulz, in charge of TeleBridge's public relations, was aghast when she saw the events of 9/11. She stormed into the office of her bosses: "I don't believe this. Turn on the TV. In New York somebody tries to imitate our spot." The people in charge watched the terrorist attacks with unbelieving eyes and open mouths. Their first thought: "Damn, we have to stop our spot! Immediately!!" But then they said to themselves that it would be a great mistake to withdraw such a visionary piece of Sindelfing trash from cir-culation. No thought wasted on the victims and casualties, only damage control.

Now it was up to visionary Sindelfing to supervise the ultimate destruction, the End of the World for this new Zanyflix series. The German director didn't hesitate to cast some well-known faces from Hubbell's Church, among them Tom, John and Will, and even asked Donald for a brief cameo appearance. Donald agreed to loan them his digital clone because when shooting was to start, he was on the golf course.

There was a company in Tinseltown that specialized in this type of digital cloning. So far, several thousand celebrities, real ones and would-be's, had been cloned by Karel who used for the scanning process the latest medical equipment from Germany.

Karel had become a master in this technique:

Digitizing people has many benefits and applications. Capturing the "real geometry" of a human provides an indisputable data set that becomes an asset which can be utilized across multiple platforms. Data can be processed and refined using a myriad of software and tools to create the "digital thespians" we see in most action sequences in feature films today. There are many different approaches and often various VFX houses will develop their own proprietary pipeline for producing their models. This includes texture capture & refinement, animation rigging and sophisticated lighting controls to simulate any environment. The tools are ever evolving, from the early laser scanners, white light grid projection to the flexibility and versatility of high-resolution camera photogrammetry. Many people we have captured are actors, pop singers, politicians, athletes and other notable celebrities. This is significant because along with their life's body of work, they leave behind 3D information that contributes to their immortality. Combined with motion and sound capture synthesis, the digital double can participate in media long after the life of the original host.

The fast progress of 3D printing has elevated the quality and authenticity of transposing digital data to the physical form in an expanding scope of materials. One day possibly living flesh and bone. This is driven by the progression of content collection. Virtual reality, augmented reality and the "4th dimension" cross the boundaries of new experiences.

Karel was sure that *it is not far in the future where AI (artificial intelligence) will be a common driver of sophisticated geometry. Today there are amazing immersive video games and films that project a clear vision of what's to come. The more that can be captured and collected, the more can be multiplied and emulated providing an almost indistinguishable reality with unpredictable outcome.*

Sindelfing's Zanyflix vision about the end of the world featured the ugliest of ghouls—spit out from Satan's abyss—and immediately was turned into an interactive environment property by Brainwaves.

Brainwaves' most recent sensation was a new computer game: *Zombies from Hell*, the hottest game in the online community. A big contest of the greatest gamers resulted in two finalists who fought for a scholar of the Brainwave Games Academy where supposedly only the best in the world were accepted.

Out of a hundred participants two kids, a boy and girl, Noodle & Sue, made the highest scores and qualified as the final *Cracks of Doom.*

The end game was going to take place at Brainwaves Headquarters, the Shangri-La of computer gamers.

Cool. The kids entered the Academy's Dragon Gate and were given the grand tour through one of the most mysterious digital academies of the world:

> *The Place Where They Dream Future.*
> *The Place Where They Explore Future.*
> *The Place Where They Turn Future into Magic.*

But the Academy was nothing more than a façade. Behind the ordinary classrooms with easy-going teachers and students in front of the obligatory computer screens there was another section, and so the three entered a new space behind the walls where virtual history was written. Here artificial intelligence and robotics, the legacy of Distler Engineering, dominated. Here human teachers retreated mysteriously and deferred to the artificial envisioning officers.

This was sheer magic—but unlike the magic of the *Harry Potter* franchise this one went without magic wands. Although established by a Teutonic Witch, it was not like that infamous School of Witchcraft and Wizardry they knew from the popular, best-selling youth novels that identified magic with medieval incantations and cursed voodoo dolls. No witch-riding, flying on brooms or boiling toads in magic cauldrons.

This here was true magic—the magic of the 21st Century and beyond.

To enter the Pleasure Island of this elite school, to apply for free scholarship the kids were told they would have to dare and travel.

"Where do we travel?"

"To the most distant place you can imagine. It's like a magic forest."

"Where is it?"

"The distant future. And one of you will return as champ of games."

"And the other one."

The artificial envision officers remained vague about that.

"His or her life will be changed too."

"And how does it work?" Sue wanted to know.

"Well, we're doing amazing things with brainwave entertainment, awareness, and expanded consciousness."

Noodle had no qualms.

"Just imagine. In a parallel world the future already exists waiting to be born. We only have to find the interface to communicate and tap it, milk knowledge for the benefit of mankind. Each traveler will return with a secret message from the future and the one that is highest valued will win. As easy as that. Find a cure to fight diseases, fight the next pandemic, make life more comfortable, kill the hunger in the world and overcome climate change."

"Above all," they were told, "this game is not horse-and-buggy and our equipment is proof: The notion of the PC as a mouse-keyboard-monitor device—in fact a TV set with a typewriter in front—is becoming archaic, isn't it? We're not working like all the other publishers who focus on games for mobile devices and social media or produce new episodes or levels that extend the life of console or PC games in the form of downloadable content. This is stone age. We don't need a PC, don't need a console anymore. We're ahead of time. What is needed is a new interface that can be tuned to future, we need ... *tam-tam*—BCI..."

"Brain-Computer interfaces?"

"Sure, a new generation of BCI. Over the last years, our researchers have started to get quite adapt at reading human brain activity and thoughts. There are advanced BCIs that can be implanted directly into your brain. It's like telepathy in a way. But our brain-computer interface is a mind-machine if there ever was one, a direct neural interface..."

"Wow!"

"...created to make magic true and authentic. And all we need are ... your personalities."

"Gosh! That sure is mind-blowing!"

"Therefore, of course, we need your scans. And if you don't mind, we need your avatar complete, physical and psychic. Your bodies will remain here in these pods, in a state of suspended animation."

"Suspended animation? Death?!" Sue is shocked.

"Not death. Certainly not brain-dead. What the hell are you thinking of! Your brain will be alive and in control, as state-of-the-art interface. You will be revived and rise from the dead in glory."

They all had a good laugh. It sounded that pathetic and melodramatic.

Sue was still skeptical about it but didn't want to make a retreat and laughed down being a coward.

While the kids' bodies were sealed inside the pods, their Avatars started into *virtual galaxies where no man had gone before.*

Their mind was using different life forms that all turned out artificial.

Noodle, half Chinese, half American, immediately boarded a giant robot that looked like a *Transformer* and surely was a virtual projection of his subconscious comic mind.

Sue transformed into a digital snake.

Thus, they entered the Age of Spiritual Machines where computers exceeded human intelligence. The future consisted of *brain total.*

No pain, no torture, no pollution, no overpopulation—but life, life eternal.

Noodle got ecstatic. He felt like God. No doubt, this was better than the proverbial magic wand. He didn't know that he was going to import a dangerous computer virus from the future that was going to annihilate life forms that command only low IQ scores.

Like Hansel and Gretel entered the witch's forest, Sue & Noodle entered Rita's digital forest.

Rita's digital clone was preparing for the kids' arrival and for—*doomsday* scheduled for April 30.

Gallery

A Rare Look Into Nazi Entertainment, 1933–1945

Two hand puppets (anti-Semitic style) carved by Theo Eggink.
Courtesy of Gerd J. Pohl.

Kasper and Devil riding a V2 rocket: Lithography for a
puppet play staged during WW2.
Courtesy of Gerd J. Pohl.

Hansel and Gretel (1940): Burn Witch Burn!
Courtesy of Schongerfilm.

Cartoon film animators working under the watchful
eyes of the "Führer".
Courtesy of J. P. Storm.

www.ingramcontent.com/pod-product-compliance
Lightning Source LLC
Chambersburg PA
CBHW051139020726
47501CB00005B/1576